The Two Sisters

P9-CCI-066

The Two Sisters

HONOR ARUNDEL

SCHOLASTIC BOOK SERVICES
New York Toronto London Auckland Sydney Tokyo

First published in Great Britain by William Heinemann Ltd.

This book is sold subject to the condition that it shall not be resold, lent, or otherwise circulated in any binding or cover other than that in which it is published—unless prior written permission has been obtained from the publisher—and without a similar condition, including this condition, being imposed on the subsequent purchaser.

ISBN: 0-590-31392-4

Copyright © 1968 by Honor Arundel. This edition is published by Scholastic Book Services, a division of Scholastic Magazines, Inc., by arrangement with Meredith Press.

18 17 16 15 14 13 12 11 10 9   01/8

Printed in the U.S.A.

1

When Maura arrived home that day after school, Mother and Dad were in the middle of one of their tremendous rows. Mum was usually even tempered, but every now and again Dad did something so awful that she blazed a real twenty-one gun salute in his direction and he blazed back and the whole house rocked. Sometimes Maura felt sorry for Dad, but mostly she felt sorry for Mum, especially now that she was old enough to understand what Mum had to put up with. On this occasion she realized from the first words she overheard as she came into the house that Dad had lost his job again. "Oh we all know you're too good for the work," she heard her mother say bitterly.

Her father was an electrician and from all accounts he was an extremely good electrician, but he could never stand the same job for long. There was always a foreman who "threw his weight around" or a boss who "treated him like a slave" or working conditions that "the Royal Society for the Prevention of Cruelty to Animals would complain about." And then he would stamp out of the place, demanding his working cards as if he were royalty and come home to tell them all about the wrongs he would never suffer again.

The trouble was that if you walk out of a job you aren't eligible for unemployment pay (b'roo money, Dad called it), but her father could never bear waiting to be fired. He liked to be the one who flounced out in a high state of indignation. So until he found another job they had to live on savings and once they even had to apply for public assistance — at least Mum did; Dad was too proud. He just could not resign himself to being a wage slave. He thought he was doing any firm a favor by working for them and that they ought to thank him ten times a day for giving them the benefit of his skill and judgment as well as paying him handsomely at the end of the week. It was all very well for him, but the person who suffered was Mum, who had been saving up for new furniture and a proper vacation ever since Maura could remember, not to speak of new clothes for her sister Caroline and herself.

Maura was particularly furious now because she had seen some fabulous shoes that she really needed and now she would have to go on wearing her old scuffed ones. So she opened the kitchen door prepared to fire a few guns herself.

Her mother was sitting at the table with an angry cold look in her eyes and Dad was striding around the room, rumpling his hair with dramatic gestures and his eyes flashing with indignation. Maura guessed he'd had two or three whiskies on the way home — he usually did when he walked out of a job.

"He's just a wee stuffy," Dad spluttered contemptuously, talking, Maura supposed, about the

6

foreman or the works manager, "thinking he can lay down the law to Dennis Cafferty and him without two thoughts in his brain to rub together and produce a spark."

"If you're so great, why aren't *you* the foreman?" sneered Mum.

"Foreman — I wouldn't be a foreman for all the gold at the foot of the rainbow. I'll never be a boss's man if I live to be a hundred and forty."

"There's no danger of you doing that. You're more likely to die of overwork, I don't think," said Mum sarcastically.

"I'm not afraid of work," retorted Dad. "Sure I was always the boy who could do eight hours' work in three, but respect — I must have respect. When Mr. Simpson approaches me and says, 'Cafferty,' 'Mr. Cafferty to you,' says I. 'How was it you was two and three quarters minutes late this afternoon?' says he. 'Sure I was eating smoked salmon and *coq au vin* with the Duchess of Portobelly at the North British Hotel,' says I. 'I must have punctuality,' says he. 'Has the work been done to your satisfaction or not?' says I. 'There's never been any complaints about your work,' says he, 'but punctuality,' he says, 'is the courtesy of kings.' 'And since when was I a king?' says I. 'This is a very sudden accession to the throne. I don't see me crown and scepter at all,' says I. 'Cafferty,' says he. 'Mr. Cafferty,' says I. 'Mr. Cafferty, I'm not asking you, I'm telling you. If you come back after lunch at half-past two instead of half-past one you'll get your severance.' 'I'll save you the trouble,' says I. 'Give me my severance right away. I'm not one to be insulted by some little jumped-up stuffed shirt who'd set his own pinkie on fire to light the boss's cigarette. I've independent blood in my veins,' says I."

"That's fine for your family," said Mum, as soon as she could get a word in. "Independent blood is just what we all need, better than shoes for Maura and a blazer for Caroline. I can easily pay the grocer with independent blood."

"Do you want to turn me into a creepy-crawly who wouldn't say boo to a boss?" accused Dad.

"You can say boo all you want, but get your paycheck first. Or your b'roo money if that's all you're capable of."

"Money, money, money, that's all you think of. What about me immortal soul?"

"Your immortal soul'll still need sausages for breakfast."

"Sassidge, you can keep your sassidge. I've some spirit in me still."

In spite of being so furious Maura couldn't help being fascinated. She could just see that foreman, a wee pink bald man with protruding teeth and a stammer, offering the boss a light from his own little finger. Caroline was fascinated too. She listened with wide eyes and her mouth a little open, still at the age when she believed Dad was the greatest man on earth and that every word he uttered was gospel truth. But Maura only believed about one word in ten because she knew his way of exaggerating and dramatizing everything that happened to him. He said it was his Irish blood and when he got worked up he always became very Irish, which

Maura thought was stupid because he'd been born in Scotland and lived there all his life. And he always quoted that bit about the sassidge because it came from one of his favorite plays by the Irish writer, Sean O'Casey.

Now, of course, he burst into song:

> "And burst in twain the galling chain
> And set auld Ireland free."

"Auld Ireland'll get on fine without your help, but your daughters won't."

Dad's Irishness always annoyed Maura, and so did his habit of bursting into song, so now she joined in. "But I've got to have new shoes; just look at these, Mum."

"Show them to your father, dear, he's the universal provider."

For a second Dad looked abashed, as well he might because her shoes were a disgrace.

"You'll have your new shoes," he muttered; "just give the old man a chance. I'll have a new job lined up before you can say Paddy O'Shea."

"I need them now."

Maura had to admit that when Dad was working he earned good money and was always very generous to them, and she didn't have to twist his arm much when she wanted new clothes. But it was April and all her winter clothes were dowdy and old-fashioned, and her friends were beginning to blossom out in new outfits while she was looking like a positive scarecrow. Besides, he was obsessed about her doing well at school and going to university, and since most of her teachers thought she would easily get a

9

place, Maura felt she had fulfilled her part of the bargain. It was dreary still being at school when you were seventeen (nearly eighteen) and having to wear a dull uniform. The least Dad could do was to provide nice things for her to wear out of school. So she didn't feel sympathetic toward his troubles at all. She glared at him.

He turned to Caroline and drew her close to him and kissed the top of her head.

"But you believe in your old Dad, don't you, me darlin'?" he said plaintively.

This made Maura absolutely sick, so she left them to it and went into her room. How marvelous it would be if someone suddenly gave her two hundred pounds to spend on clothes. She'd have print dresses and corduroy dresses and plain dresses in white and purple and green. She'd have lots of really well-tailored slacks with dozens of different shirts and sweaters to wear with them, a shiny scarlet raincoat, a white wool summer coat, and dozens and dozens of pairs of stockings. But what she had set her heart on was a gorgeous fur coat. She'd seen a picture of one in a magazine, with a loose belt and a hood, made in cloudy gray fur that they said was as light as swansdown. How she hated wearing a white blouse and a tie and a shabby blazer! She took them off, hurled them across the floor, and put on her housecoat because there wasn't a thing she wanted to wear. Two hundred pounds indeed! Now Dad had lost his job she wouldn't even be able to buy a handkerchief until he'd got a new job, and by that time there'd be debts to be paid. Mum couldn't bear owing anyone a penny.

Other people's fathers worked steadily at the same job for years and years, Maura thought resentfully, and saved up for vacations and furniture. Dad was almost forty, yet he was still as wild and irresponsible as he had been, according to Mum, at twenty. He was always flouncing out of jobs and taking days off and talking about his rights. And then he would suddenly spend money like water on some boring book he wanted them all to read — once he had nearly bought a whole set of encyclopedias, for instance, but fortunately Mum had managed to stop him in time. Or a picture for the hall — naturally it was Van Gogh's stupid sunflowers, sneered Maura — or a telescope so that they could study the stars, all at a time when Caroline needed a new raincoat, when she needed underclothes, and poor Mum was in rags.

Dad was always going on about the importance of education — just because he had had to leave school at fourteen. In actual fact, he was quite intelligent and had read as many books as the English teacher, and he could recite poetry by the hour. But he could not forget that he was one of the "underprivileged classes." Maura thought all this class business was stupid. People were just people.

Anyhow the result was that he nagged Caroline and herself over their homework and was always dragging them off to art galleries, museums, and ancient monuments, and saying, "A person should never stop learning. It's never too early and it's never too late." It was lucky for Maura that she was moderately clever, but she felt embarrassed when Dad marveled at her

11

knowledge of Latin, French, and math and kept saying almost incredulously, "To think that a daughter of mine should be able to go to university." At school prizegivings he turned up in his best dark suit with a glittering white shirt, boring everyone for miles around by telling them how clever his daughter was. She used to dread bringing her report cards home, because a girl couldn't work hard all the time and when some teacher wrote, "Does very well when she applies herself" or "Good, but should work harder," Dad would nearly explode. Fortunately she found that by last-minute cramming she could usually do well in exams, and that satisfied him more or less. He certainly enjoys prizegivings more than I do, Maura thought. How I loathe tripping onto the platform and curtsying to some fat woman who is wearing a stupid hat and a stupid smile!

Of course it was nice to do well, but she wasn't really ambitious and sometimes she did not even know if she wanted to go to university. Edinburgh was full of students, all wearing huge scarves and shaggy coats and they looked as though they were enjoying themselves, but the thought of poring over books and passing more exams depressed her. Still, it might be fun to be part of a crowd of talented, interesting people, and talk and drink coffee and meet exciting men. She could not bear boys of her own age, but surely some of them would have grown up by then. And it would be nice to have a few extra years of gay, carefree youth before the treadmill or the rat race absorbed her forever.

Maura heard the front door slam and guessed that Dad had gone out to the pub. He usually did at moments of stress, and when he came home he would move and speak very slowly and carefully so that no one would guess that he was drunk.

Maura rolled herself off the bed; she decided to have a bath and wash her hair before tea.

The bath was a splendid place for thinking, but she found that instead of thoughts about clothes or school or her future plans she was still thinking about her father. She used to think he was marvelous when she was little; he used to tell her fairy stories which he made up out of his head and sing Scottish and Irish folk songs by the hour, and she always used to believe that one day they would do the unlikely things he wanted to do, like traveling around the world in a cargo boat or living in a lighthouse or a Mediterranean villa or running an antique shop or an orange grove.

Probably Caroline still did believe Dad, thought Maura, lazily soaping herself.

And how she used to love their expeditions to the country. Her grandparents had come to Scotland after the First World War to work in the potato harvest as potato pickers, and then her grandfather had become a gardener and, according to Dad, grew the best roses in the country. Dad had nearly become a gardener himself, only he hated being polite to the gentry, so he had become an electrician instead. But he had never forgotten his country upbringing and he loved to show them how to find wild strawberries and hazel nuts and mushrooms when they went for walks. Maura used to be so surprised when he would suddenly stop and pounce into the hedgerow to pick a wild strawberry — she thought he must be a magician.

But now she was no longer a child and fairy tales bored her, folk songs gave her a pain, and when Dad started talking about living in a country cottage or running an orange grove in Spain she just yawned. Because there they were, still in this horrible, old-fashioned apartment with the furniture falling to bits; they hardly ever had a vacation, let alone a trip abroad, and she couldn't imagine, as long as Dad went on walking out of jobs, that anything could ever be different.

By this time she was out of the bath. She put her hair in rollers and stuck her bangs down with the tape just as Mum called to her that tea was ready.

And Maura thought, Yes, I must go to university. I must get a good degree and then I'll find a fabulous job with long, long vacations, live in a super modern apartment, and have closets filled with delicious clothes.

Somehow she always got back to clothes.

2

The next day was Caroline's birthday. The April sun poked through the gap in her bedroom curtains and picked out a bright patch on her pillow; then it moved to her face. She woke up. The first thing she remembered was that it was her birthday. She was nine years old.

Her mother knocked on the door. "Caroline, time to get up," she called and put a smiling face round the door. "And many happy returns."

Caroline slid out of bed and then she raised her arms, breathed in the early morning air, and did a little dance on the cold floor. It was lovely to start a new day and she could never understand why Maura stayed in bed till the last minute, groaning under a mound of bedclothes as if she were drowning and only staggering out after the third call from her mother.

Caroline went into the bathroom, still in her bare feet, to brush her teeth. She looked at herself in the mirror.

"I'm nine," she told her reflection. "I'm quite different from what I was yesterday."

The face in the mirror looked back: eyes like Daddy's that sometimes looked green-brown and sometimes looked golden, a snub nose with a shower of freckles, dark untidy hair. There was no difference that she could see.

While she dressed herself she remembered last night's quarrel and wondered if it had been solved after she had gone to bed. Mum's face had looked cheerful, certainly, but that might have just been because of her birthday. If only Daddy had not walked out of his job, and yet it couldn't have been his fault because he was so clever. Everyone said so. He knew all the answers to her questions and the right way to do anything from papering a room to fixing the electric iron, and one day, when she was older, they would do some of the exciting things he was always planning. The plan that appealed to her most was to live in the country and have their own garden. Although they lived in an upstairs apartment without any garden at all she felt she already knew all about gardening from her father. She could remember Granny's cottage garden and the garden of the big house where Grandpa used to work with its walled kitchen gardens, smooth lawns, and rose-planted terraces falling away to a lake as round and pale as a plate. So when Daddy talked about gardens she imagined a combination of the two, adding the huge beech hedge and the banks of daffodils from the Botanic Gardens where they sometimes walked on Sundays.

"We'll have an orchard, Caroline, and plant daffodils and narcissi," Daddy would say. "And I rather fancy some clematis, the dark purple sort, climbing up a trellis, and we'll have roses, loads and loads of roses." He would draw little

16

pictures and argue endlessly about the virtues of box or beech hedge, lavender and fuchsia bushes, white and purple lilac. They would pore over gardening catalogs together. Caroline, like Daddy, preferred the old-fashioned names like sweet William, love-in-a-mist, columbine, and marigold to the complicated Latin names in the catalogs. "*Coreopsis, nemesia,*" he would say in disgust. "They don't sound like flowers, they sound like diseases. Please, Doctor, I think I have a slight touch of *nemesia.*" Perhaps now Daddy would find a new job in the country and then they'd be able to have a real garden of their own.

In the kitchen, breakfast was ready — golden toast in the toast rack, a brown boiled egg in a blue-and-white striped eggcup, a stream of golden tea flowing into her cup, yellow butter on a plate, orange marmalade in a pot. Beside her plate was a pile of crunchy brown paper parcels.

"Eat your breakfast before you open them," said Mum.

"How's my birthday girl?" asked Daddy, giving her a hug.

"Birthday," mumbled Maura, pouring sugar onto her cornflakes.

Caroline ate her egg in delicate spoonfuls and bit off neat little half moons of crisp toast and soft butter and drank her tea. In between she watched them all with quick birdlike glances to see if last night's quarrel had been made up. Maura was no guide; she was always sleepy at breakfast and never talked much. Mum was brisk and tidy in a flowered housedress, pouring tea and smiling. Daddy was in shirt sleeves, opening

17

his egg with one expert stroke of his knife. But instead of smelling fragrantly of shaving soap and with his hair still damp above his ears, he was lounging in his weekend trousers and his open-necked shirt, unshaven and crumpled. Instead of collecting his lunch box and filling his thermos with tea, he was leaning back in his chair, lighting a cigarette. It was his expression, however, that made Caroline realize that the quarrel was still going on; he had a guilty look which he was trying to hide behind a don't-care-ish gaiety. And though both Daddy and Mum were talking affectionately to her, neither was speaking to the other. Caroline sighed and began to open her parcels.

The first one was a green turtlenecked sweater, a present from her parents. The next one was a pin, a silver horse with a very curly mane, from Maura. There was a package of silly handkerchiefs embroidered with tiny flowers from Aunt Maggie and a money order for five shillings from Granny.

"Thank you, oh thanks," she murmured, kissing her Daddy and Mum and giving a special grin to Maura. "I wish I could wear the pin to school but I'll take it to show to the girls."

"Green as the shamrock for an Irish lass," said her father in his special Irish voice which Caroline loved because it usually meant he was in a good mood. But now he was doing it to prove that everything was all right when it quite clearly wasn't.

Oh dear, thought Caroline, why must they be like this on my birthday? She went into her bedroom and put her green sweater in her drawer and her silver pony pin into a very safe part of her school satchel. She collected her lunch tickets, looked to see if there were any egg marks at the corners of her mouth and poked her head into the kitchen.

"Bye," she said to everyone.

"Good-bye," said her mother with false brightness.

"Bye bye, me darlin' girl," said her father.

Maura was in the bathroom doing frantic last-minute things to her hair before she too went to school, but one did not say good-bye to sisters.

Caroline set off in a divided state of mind, part of her still remembering her happy waking-up birthday feeling and part of her worried about her parents. She hated fights and people shouting at each other and not feeling sure whose side she ought to be on.

She had two ways of going to school. If it was raining she took a bus that skirted the Meadows, a flat, green, open space fringed with trees. But if it was fine she preferred to walk along the path at the near side of the Meadows, between an avenue of trees, until she came out near Tollcross where her school was. This took about ten minutes extra but it meant that she could spend her bus money on a bar of chocolate or a package of potato chips or a slab of sticky toffee.

She chose to walk today because the sun was shining through the trees, making speckly patterns on the path. The hawthorn hedge was a bright tender green and the air smelled cool and delicious. She watched the plum-colored buses bowling along and an old man with a spiked stick collecting the paper and cigarette cartons left by messy people. Dogs chased each other on the grass and a group of big high school girls giggled and gossiped a few yards ahead.

At Tollcross there were two big sandstone pillars which looked as though someone had started to build a triumphal arch and then had suddenly become bored halfway through. Caroline had seen them hundreds of times before, but today for the first time she noticed that on top of the pillars were the heads of unicorns. There was no mistaking the horn sticking out of the grubby standstone head. Caroline stopped and stared. What on earth was a unicorn doing on top of a pillar at the entrance to the Meadows? Did it like white bread or brown? Or plum cake? She must ask Daddy. He would be certain to know.

When she got to school she stopped thinking about unicorns because her best friend, Jean, had brought her a box of chocolates and her second-best friend, Elspeth, had brought her a pocket comb in its own little case.

"Many happy returns!" they chorused, thumping her on the back nine times.

Caroline reeled under the blows and wished that Jean hadn't given her chocolates. It meant passing them around. Still, it would be abominably greedy to gobble them all herself, so she opened the box and handed it around. To her horror Jean took her favorite kind, a chocolate caramel. She shut the box quickly and put it into her satchel.

"Look what my big sister's given me," she said, "a pony pin."

"Is it real silver?"

"I guess it is, sort of."

When Caroline got home from school her father was sitting in the kitchen reading poetry, which he often did in moments of stress. Caroline liked it too, even when she could not understand it properly.

"Listen to this," he said.

> "Though I am old with wandering
> Through hollow lands and hilly lands,
> I shall find out where she has gone,
> And kiss her lips and take her hands;
> And walk among long dappled grass,
> And pluck till time and times are done
> The silver apples of the moon,
> The golden apples of the sun."

Caroline listened. Dappled grass was what she had been walking on this morning on her way to school and the silver apples and the golden apples reminded her of their imaginary orchard.

"How's my birthday girl?"

"I'm fine, Daddy. Jean gave me some chocolates and Elspeth gave me a bug rake."

"A what?"

"A comb. Everyone calls them bug rakes."

"It's a fine expression to come from a wee lassie."

"But everyone does."

"The Caffertys don't have to be like everyone else," said her father haughtily.

"Where's Mum?"

"Out," said her father shortly. "But I'll make you some tea. We'll have it together, just the two of us. Maura said she'd be late."

Caroline loved having tea alone with Daddy.

She liked watching him get it ready; he was so deft and precise in all his movements. He swirled the boiling water in the teapot to warm it in a special way and he always laid the knives diagonally across the plates. His eyes, which had crackled with anger last night, were glowing and gentle, and he smiled a warm, companionable smile.

"I've made some hot buttered toast," he said, opening the oven door and drawing out a plate piled high with golden, buttery toast. "We'll eat it with strawberry jam and see, I've remembered it's your birthday and found a cake."

It was a white cake, bought in a shop, but he had stuck nine pink candles on it which he now lit with a flick of his cigarette lighter.

Caroline sat down and began to eat hungrily.

"Daddy," she said through a mouthful of toast and strawberry jam, "why are there unicorns in the Meadows?"

"Unicorns in the Meadows? Are there now? Well, it would seem the right place for them."

"They're on pillars," explained Caroline.

"The poor creatures."

"Do you suppose," asked Caroline, knowing that this was just the sort of question Daddy loved to answer, "that there are any live ones left in Scotland?"

"Not many I shouldn't think," said her father, taking a gulp of tea and smiling. "But there used to be hundreds before there were so many houses. They used to roam the Pentland Hills and then in the winter they'd come to the city for food and shelter. No one was supposed actually to see them, so people left bundles of grass in the Grassmarket and the unicorns would tiptoe in at midnight to find it."

"Is that true, Daddy?" Caroline asked severely.

"Why wouldn't it be?" he answered.

"And the ones I saw?"

"They have to sit on their pillars except on special days like the first of May and Midsummer Day and New Year's Eve, and then at midnight they jump down and scamper about the Meadows until sunrise."

"Go on." Caroline loved this. She didn't care if it was true or not.

"They're terribly shy, unicorns, and can't bear people seeing them, except perhaps occasionally wee girls like you. And they hate houses and streets, they only like fields and gardens."

"Do you think I'll ever see one?"

"I shouldn't be a bit surprised."

"Do you think we'll ever have a garden?"

Her father's glowing eyes clouded slightly. With an effort he said, "But of course. We'll have a great garden, you and me, an orchard with silver apples and golden apples and Michaelmas daisies and peonies. At this time of year there'd be a sea of daffodils." His voice trailed away. "We might walk in the Botanic Gardens on the weekend."

"Let's," said Caroline quickly.

"Time you attacked your birthday cake."

Caroline shut her eyes, took an enormous breath and huffed and puffed until all the candles had been blown out. Then she took the bread knife and began to cut the first slice.

"Have you wished?" asked her father.

Caroline shut her eyes. "I wish, I wish," she said silently — but what? A garden? Daddy having a new job? Everyone being nice again?

At that very moment her mother came in and at first glance Caroline could see that at least one part of her wish had not been granted — Mum was still in last night's mood. Daddy pretended not to notice.

"Sit down, love," he said cheerily, "and have a cuppa tea and a slice of birthday cake, and will I make you some toast?"

"How was school?" Mum asked, ignoring him but accepting the cup of tea.

"It was fine. Jean gave me some chocolates and Elspeth gave me a bug — a comb."

"Don't eat them all at once," her mother said mechanically, only hearing the word chocolates.

"Daddy's been telling me about unicorns," began Caroline, anxious to fill the silence.

"He's no business to be filling your head with nonsense."

"It's not nonsense, Mum."

"The trouble with your father is that he believes his own fairy tales, and you're just as bad. Fairy tales are just an excuse for not facing facts."

Caroline glanced quickly at her father who colored deeply and lit a cigarette.

"Fairy tales are a way of facing facts," he muttered through a cloud of smoke. He looked as though he were going to continue speaking and then turned away to look out of the window.

"But there are unicorns in the Meadows," persisted Caroline, determined to defend Daddy.

"Unicorns are part of the coat of arms of Scotland," said her mother scornfully. "I thought everyone knew that. Lions for England and unicorns for Scotland."

"Oh," said Caroline limply.

"Sitting at home reading poetry and telling fairy tales while his wife has to go out to work," continued Mum, triumphantly.

"To work?" Dad was astonished.

"Well, someone has to work in this family. So I got myself a job. I'm not too proud to soil my hands with honest toil."

"What sort of a job?" Dad asked evenly.

"Serving in a café down the street. Ten till four."

"You'd no business to take a job without telling me."

"I never noticed you asking my permission before you walked out of yours."

"That was different."

"I don't see the difference."

"I'm the breadwinner of this family," said Daddy, beginning to shout.

"Delighted to hear it, I'm sure."

"I've always been able to provide for my family and I'll go on doing so as long as my strength holds out."

"Hullo, what's all the shouting about?" Maura came into the kitchen, dropping her school bag on the floor and shaking her hair loose.

Her father looked up furiously.

"I've taken a job," said her mother.

"Good for you, Mum," said Maura, with a smile for her mother and a spiteful glance for her father.

Caroline watched them with a painful feeling of involvement. One minute she and Daddy had been so happy and close together, eating buttered toast and talking, and now —

"I've my homework to do," she said desperately and rushed out of the room. Why do they? Why do they? she asked herself as she went into her room. She heard more voices raised and then the front door slammed. Daddy had gone out. Then there was a long, low-voiced conversation between Mum and Maura but she could not hear what they were saying. She did not really want to hear. She shut her door and took out her books. She had wanted to put on her new green sweater and her pony pin but now she hadn't the heart.

"Everything's horrible," she told George, her teddy bear. "Nobody should be horrible on my birthday."

3

Maura sat talking to Mum for a long time, or rather letting her mother do the talking. Mum was feeling proud of herself for having found a job because it meant she had won round two of her battle with Dad. She was now the breadwinner and the idea excited her. Frankly, working in a smelly café made Maura shudder with disgust. Imagine having to scrape congealed food off dirty plates and bawl out "fried fish for two" and "egg and chips for one." But then poor Mum had never had any training for anything. She had married Dad at a fantastically early age when she was working in a food-canning factory and she had been a housewife ever since. If Maura had to take a summer job she would never work in a café. In fact she and her friend Linda had put their names down for Marks and Spencers Department Store because they gave a handsome discount on their clothes. There was always a waiting list because they wanted what they called "a better class of girl," which meant that one had to look clean and well-dressed and not speak gutter-Scots or chew gum. So Maura and Linda were keeping their fingers crossed.

At the same time as she was feeling proud of

herself, Mum was obviously worried and a little guilty.

"I did want us to have a proper vacation this year," she said. "If only your father gets another job quickly."

"He's sure to," Maura said unconvincingly. Once he had been unemployed for three months and they had eaten nothing but kippers and baked beans for weeks and no one could have any new clothes.

"It would happen on Caroline's birthday," her mother went on, "and she oughtn't to be upset by things like this."

"Caroline's all right," Maura said. "She's tougher than you think and anyhow she lives in a little world of her own. She tells her troubles to that revolting teddy bear and then forgets them."

"She was having such a nice birthday tea with Dad, both of them talking nonsense as usual, and I spoiled it all."

"It wasn't your fault, it was Dad's" Maura said, getting up from her chair.

"I know but — could you look in on her on your way to bed, Maura?"

"Sure," Maura said, as she left the room.

She opened Caroline's door and called her name softly.

"Hullo," she answered.

"Aren't you asleep yet?"

"I am, almost."

Maura switched on the light and there she was, lying in bed with half a dozen books on top of her and this sordid teddy bear she insisted upon sleeping with. Maura took the books away and piled them beside her on the floor.

"Do you really need this animal?" she asked.

"It's not an animal; he's George."

Maura could tell from her eyes, unfocused and vague, that Caroline was miles away, so she just said comfortingly, "Everything's going to be all right. Good night, Carol."

Maura undressed and got into bed and then decided to read for half an hour to take her mind off things. She was reading *Jane Eyre* and had just got to the terrifically sad part when Jane runs away from Mr. Rochester and is lying on the cold moor. Hardly anyone at school read books — they just read magazines — so Maura always felt a bit snobbish if she admitted to reading books like *Jane Eyre* or *The Mill on the Floss* for fun. Of course she liked magazines too, especially for the fashions, but the stories were stupid. There was no point in reading a story you knew beforehand would work out happily. She liked stories to be sad, too, but in any case the important thing was not to know what the ending would be. She was pretty sure *Jane Eyre* would finish happily but she could not be absolutely certain. Nowadays, she reflected, Mr. Rochester would have been able to divorce his mad wife, but she didn't mind books being old-fashioned, and she loved dark, inscrutable, difficult heroes like Mr. Rochester and Mr. Darcy and Heathcliff. Why did she never meet anyone remotely like them in real life?

Maura liked poetry too, but there again most of the people at school would faint if she admitted to learning "Ode to a Nightingale" for pleasure or told them how some of the speeches in *Macbeth* gave her cold shivers down her spine. They just looked at English literature as something to pass exams with. What Maura hated were the essays she was told to write — "Is Macbeth a Tragic Hero?" for instance, or "The Position of Women in the Victorian Novel," which did not seem to bear any relation to what she felt when she read *Macbeth* or *Jane Eyre*. Perhaps it would be different when she went to the university.

By the time she had got Jane properly rescued by Diana and Mary she had forgotten all about Mum and Dad and Caroline, and promptly fell asleep.

But in the morning the first thing she noticed was that Dad's place hadn't been set and that Mum looked as though she'd been crying.

"Where's Dad?" she asked as casually as she could.

"He's gone out," Mum said evasively.

"When's he coming back?" demanded Caroline in an alarmed voice.

"Soon, dear," replied Mum, but with a certain hesitation, Maura thought.

Maura felt alarmed too. Suppose he'd left them; that would really be the last straw. The moment Caroline had gone upstairs to get ready for school she asked, "Didn't Dad say where he was going?"

"Not a thing."

"But when did he go?"

"He wasn't there when I woke up." Mum's

voice trembled. "Maura, it was my fault. I said some cruel things to him. I lost my temper."

"He had no business to leave his job," Maura said angrily. That meant Dad had won round three of the battle, and so unfairly too, just by walking out of the house.

"He has every right," said Mum, giving up completely. "It's his life. And his self-respect is so important to him."

"Self-respect!" Maura sniffed.

Mum looked pale and her eyes — she had beautiful gray eyes with long, dark lashes — filled with tears and she gripped Maura's hand for a minute and then released it, trying unsuccessfully to smile.

Maura stopped feeling angry and felt sorry for her mother instead.

"He'll be back, Mum, don't worry," she said as comfortingly as she could.

"Of course he will."

But she didn't sound very convincing.

"I hope your job goes well. I must fly."

Maura did not often kiss her mother but suddenly she felt older and wiser and extremely protective, so she put an arm around her and kissed her cheek which was always smooth and cool and nice-smelling. Then she raced for the bus because, except during the bus strike, which hadn't been her fault, she was in the proud position of never having been late for school in her life.

All that day at school her thoughts kept wandering away from the causes of industrial unrest in Britain after the Napoleonic Wars, Ovid's boring exile by the Black Sea, or the three unities as exemplified in the plays of Racine to what could have happened to Dad. It was just possible that he could have run off and put one of his wild ambitions into practice. He might be on a cargo boat bound for the West Indies or on a whaler bound for the Arctic Circle.

She wanted badly to confide in her friend Linda but she did not dare; somehow to put her fears into words would have made them more real. So when Linda asked why she was so silent, she said offhand, "Oh, family fights as usual."

"Your family does lead a rich emotional life," said Linda enviously.

"Well, I don't happen to care for kitchen-sink drama," Maura said morosely.

"It's better than being bored. My parents never even speak to each other; Dad grunts and Mum sighs and then — curtain."

Linda was Maura's special friend, six weeks older than Maura and already eighteen, with silvery blond hair, a slightly crooked nose, and a deep gurgling laugh that was constantly getting her into trouble because the teachers could always recognize it. She was a natural actress and always played the lead in school plays; and she would convulse her friends by imitating the lady supervisor complaining about "boy and gel relationships" or the headmaster growling over a bad report or the history teacher, who was an ardent Scottish Nationalist, describing the Act of Union in 1707 as a "marriage of convenience, involving financial swindle and legal rape."

Linda was hoping to go to university too, though Maura told her she ought to go to drama school. Linda's parents, however, had set their hearts on her going into the civil service and they thought acting was next door to striptease. In any case, even if she did become a proper actress, it was always a good idea to have a regular mealticket to fall back on, since the Labor Exchange was not so generous as the Ministry of Agriculture and Fisheries. Linda thought Maura had very mature ideas.

"What was the fight about?" Linda repeated as they walked each other to the shop to buy chips and chocolate to supplement what they considered a meager lunch. "Or do you want to keep your family skeletons in their cupboards?"

"Dad walked out of his job again," Maura said.

"Good for him."

"What do you mean? It's not good for us."

"I like to hear of individual initiative in the older generation."

Maura took a swipe at her friend.

"Look at it from a man's point of view," Linda went on. "How would you like to have to go to a dreary job for the rest of your life because one day, twenty years ago, in a fit of romantic weakness, you asked some girl to marry you?" Maura could not help laughing, but she was still worried underneath and she did not go for coffee with Linda after school as she often did. She dashed out of school and pushed a lot of squawling juniors to one side so that she could get a place on the first bus.

"If he's abandoned us I'll never forgive him, never, never, never," she thought. "Mum will have to work full time in a steamy stinking café and I'll have to work full time in a dreary insurance office and sweat at night school to improve my qualifications. And poor Caroline will be heartbroken and probably become psychologically maladjusted and delinquent, ringing doorbells and shoplifting from Woolworth's. And none of us will ever have any new clothes again."

She ran up the stairs and then very slowly opened the flat door, willing Dad to be there. But he wasn't. Her mother and Caroline were drinking tea in the kitchen. Mum looked simply dreadful, thought Maura, at least ninety years old, her face pale and steamy from working in the hot café, wearing a shapeless skirt and down-at-heel shoes, and her hair like a bird's nest.

"Dad not back yet?" Maura asked without even a pretense at casualness.

"Not yet," said Mum, with a smile for Caroline's benefit.

"How's your job?" Maura asked with an effort.

"To tell you the truth I rather like it. It's a change from being home all day. The manageress is nice and they gave me a grand lunch, steak pie, apple crumble, and coffee."

"Gosh," said Caroline enviously, "better than our school lunch."

"What did you have?" asked Mum, because Caroline loved to describe her midday meal.

"Guess," Caroline said.

"Roast pork, apple sauce, and ice cream," said Mum — this sort of question and answer was a regular family game.

"No," shouted Caroline triumphantly. "Cold

fatty meat, lumpy mashed potato, watery cabbage, and sponge pudding with pink jam like cough medicine; it was horrible."

Maura poured herself some tea and sat down. Her heart was down somewhere near her heels and there was an aching hole where it had been. She felt really sorry for Mum, who had to go on making cheerful conversation when she must be worried rigid.

At that moment there was the sound of a key in the lock. Mum jumped to her feet and edged toward the door just as Dad bounded in and caught her in his arms.

"Dennis," she said. "Oh, Dennis."

"Daddy, where have you been?" squeaked Caroline, jumping up to be kissed and hugged. Only Maura sat still. She didn't hold with fatted calves for progidal sons or for prodigal fathers. But her heart moved up to its usual place and she felt quite faint with relief.

Her father was looking disgustingly healthy and cheerful. He bowed and presented Mum with an outsize bunch of daffodils. "For you, love," he said. "And now, pour your thirsty old Dad a cuppa tea, Caroline, and I'll tell you all my adventures."

"Where did you go, Daddy?"

"I went into the Grassmarket at dawn and there was a unicorn snuffing at the early morning air, so I leaped upon its back and it galloped off with me to fairyland."

"Typical!" Maura thought, curling her lip contemptuously, and he must have noticed because he continued in a different voice, "I went to St. Andrews Square and found a bus and I said to the conductor, 'Take me far, far away from Auld Reekie to where the sun shines, the wind blows, the daffodils are dancing under the trees, and a man can walk the green earth in freedom.'"

This was pretty nearly as bad but Caroline was so enthralled that Maura didn't interrupt.

"But where, Daddy?" Caroline persisted. "Tell us where?"

"Right down in the Borders, place called Kelso, and I walked in a ruined abbey and meditated on my sins, and then I strolled beside the silvery Tweed and rejoiced, and then I bought some cheese and some apples and walked and walked until — here I am."

"Was it lovely in the country?" Caroline asked wistfully.

"It was lovely, me darlin'. And I felt sorry for all wretched schoolgirls chained to their desks and all poor wage slaves chained to their benches and all poor housewives chained to their stoves."

"Not everyone can take a holiday just when they feel like it," Maura mumbled, half under her breath, but he must have heard. She hoped he had.

"That is why, me darlin's, I shall give you all a treat tonight. I shall take you to the pictures and follow it up with a magnificent banquet."

"That would be a fine treat, Dennis," Mum said. "I haven't been to the pictures for months and I've been longing to see *My Fair Lady*."

"Best bibs and tuckers then, my fair ladies, and be ready in half an hour."

Caroline began bouncing up and down and

Mum, smiling idiotically into Dad's face, looked all at once not ninety anymore but more like twenty-one. There was a delicate flush of pleasure on her face and her eyes sparkled. "Honestly," thought Maura, "parents are the limit! Dad loses his job, he and Mum quarrel, he disappears for twenty-four hours and drives us mad with worry, and then suddenly, hey presto, we must all celebrate and go to the pictures. What with? With the rent money or the vacation money or the money for my new shoes?"

"I can't come," she said sulkily. "I've an essay to write."

"Ach, come on, love. I'll help you with it when we come back," Dad said with his special coaxing voice. But Maura was not going to be coaxed.

"I have to work," she snarled, accenting the *I*. She stumped up to her bedroom, spread her books out on the table, and seethed with anger.

She could hear affectionate mumurs from the room next door where Dad and Mum were changing to go out. Mum was saying, "I'm sorry, Dennis, it was all my fault," and Dad was replying, "I'm a rapscallion to treat you so," followed by a long silence which probably meant they were kissing. Maura shuddered with disgust. Why should Mum have to apologize? It wasn't her fault at all. Caroline in her room was alternately banging drawers and calling out happily, "How do I look?"

They shouted good-bye but Maura did not answer. She began her essay on the causes of the Franco-Prussian War.

4

Caroline loved going out with her parents in the evening, especially when Daddy was in a mood for celebration. Caroline held his hand tightly and proudly, and took a little hop every few steps to keep up, as they walked up the street toward the movies.

"We are a good-looking family, to be sure," said Daddy, beaming at them both.

Caroline beamed back. She wasn't so sure about herself, although she was wearing her new green sweater with the silver horse pin pinned to the neck where it would show under her coat; but Mum looked splendid in her gray wool dress and her good gray coat. And as for Daddy, in his dark suit and white shirt, he was the handsomest man in Scotland.

He generously bought chocolate and popcorn and insisted on the best seats, and she sat between her parents happily munching, while they commented in low voices on the stupid advertisements before the big film began.

Caroline did not think the advertisements were stupid. She longed to lick that super new ice cream or to ride in that sleek scarlet car, or to crunch that chocolate or to sample the savorily smoking stew. She licked her lips and took another handful of popcorn.

When the big film began all conversation stopped except for Daddy occasionally turning to her and saying, "Are you enjoying it, my love?" and she replying, "Oh yes, Daddy, it's super." It was lovely to sit in the dark scented theater, watching the enormous brightly lit screen where such gorgeous people wore such gorgeous clothes and behaved so strangely and romantically. She laughed when Daddy laughed and at moments of crisis gripped his hand.

When they came out blinking into the lobby, Daddy said, "Hold on, you two, for a minute!" and disappeared into the street. Caroline and her mother spent the time looking at the photographs of all the film stars and deciding which ones they liked best, until Daddy reappeared carrying an armful of parcels.

"My ladyships, the carriage awaits," he said, and there, to Caroline's delight, was a taxi ticking away outside.

"Dennis, you shouldn't" Mum said delightedly.

"Nonsense, nothing but the best for my two fairy princesses."

"Can I sit on the little seat?" asked Caroline.

The taxi, smelling cozily of leather, purred away through the lighted streets until it drew up outside the house where they lived.

Daddy bounced out onto the pavement and paid the driver from a lordly handful of silver. Then helping Caroline and Mum out as if they were the most important people in the world, he led the way upstairs.

"Now we shall have our feast," he said, as he put the parcels of fish and chips on the kitchen table, along with two bottles of Guinness and two Cokes. "Venison pastry and stuffed boar's head, syllabubs and champagne."

Caroline felt dizzy with happiness. This was how her birthday ought to have been, she thought as she looked at the plum-colored Coke fizzing in her glass, the black creamy Guinness in her parents' glasses, the crisp golden fish on their bed of chips, sharp with vinegar and coarse kitchen salt.

"Maura," shouted Daddy gaily at the kitchen door, "come and join the feast."

There was a moment before Maura appeared, looking fragile and sleepy in a blue housecoat.

"How's my clever girl? Finished your essay? We brought you . . ." His voice trailed off as he saw the expression on her face.

"Thanks, but I don't accept presents from the unemployed," said Maura bitterly.

"Maura!" exclaimed Mum's horrified voice.

Daddy stared at Maura. His face reddened and then went pale; he struggled to speak or perhaps to prevent himself from speaking. Caroline thought that she would remember that moment forever; the expression on Maura's face, cruel and yet frightened, and her father's silence which was worse than if he had spoken. She gulped and wanted to cry, and the mouthful of fish and chips clogged into a solid lump that she could not swallow.

"Maura, go to your room," said Mum, in a voice that no one ever disobeyed.

Maura went.

Then Mum leaned toward Daddy and put a hand on his knee as if she were telling him something that couldn't be expressed in words. She began eating again, praising the freshness of the fish and the crispness of the chips with more enthusiasm than was strictly necessary.

Caroline watched Daddy. She longed, too, to put her hand on his knee and to say something, anything, to comfort him, but she did not dare.

After a minute or two of gazing somberly into space, he took a drink of Guinness and a mouthful of fish and began to talk about the film, singing snatches of the songs and telling them how he would have behaved if he had been Professor Higgins and had had the chance of winning the affections of someone as appealing as Eliza. Nevertheless it was clear to Caroline that his mind was on other things and she was glad to be soon packed off to bed.

5

The next day was Saturday and Maura slept late as usual and then lay reading, waiting for Dad to go out, because after last night she didn't want to meet him face to face. She didn't feel exactly sorry but she was beginning to have twinges of uneasiness. After a bit she put on her housecoat and started experimenting with some new eye makeup in front of her mirror.

Caroline burst into the room, as usual forgetting to knock.

"Maura, we're going to the country tomorrow," she spluttered. "Isn't it super? A professor's driving us. Daddy's going to electrify his cottage."

"What on earth are you talking about?" Maura asked sourly.

"Daddy met a professor in Kelso."

"Oh, he's always meeting people."

"I know. But this man's a professor at the university and he's got a cottage and wants Daddy to help him with the wiring. So Daddy said he didn't do Sunday work —"

"You're telling me."

" — because he liked being with his family. So the professor said we could come too. And he's calling for us tomorrow at nine o'clock and we're to take a picnic lunch."

Maura turned back to her mirror. "I'm not going to traipse around the country after Dad. The professor will think he's mad, lugging his family about with him. Besides, Sunday's the day I do my clothes and clean my room."

Caroline's face drooped. "Do come," she pleaded. "It'll be fun. A picnic lunch — you know you like picnic lunches."

"Not this Sunday. I've promised to spend the afternoon with Linda. If only Dad would give us a bit of time to think things over."

Caroline bit her lip. She could not get used to the idea that now that Maura was seventeen and nearly grown up, she was bored by family outings.

"Daddy's got a new job," she said, looking at her sister sharply to see if this would make any difference, "starting on Monday."

"When did he tell you?"

"Just now."

Maura was about to make an acid comment, but realized that she should not involve Caroline in her private dispute with her father, she said, as politely as possible, "Well, I can't come. Sorry."

Caroline trailed slowly out of the room and Maura heard her father asking, "Well?" and Caroline replying, "She says she's too busy."

For a moment Maura felt guilty. She knew she ought to go and say she was sorry or put her arms around his neck and say, "How lovely to be going into the country," or even just give him a quick pleased look and say nothing, but somehow none of these things seemed possible. Because she was still angry and the anger was like that sliver of ice in the ice maiden's heart which would not melt. Instead she thought, "How cruel of him not to tell us before. He had a new job lined up all the time and let Mother and me suffer quite unnecessarily. He doesn't deserve to be forgiven, not just yet. If he thinks he can win me over with bunches of daffodils and visits to the movies and fish suppers, he's wrong. That may work with Mum, but it doesn't work with me."

She really did spend Sundays tidying her room and doing her clothes, but she liked doing it very slowly and gradually. And this meant that she would wander around the house in her housecoat for quite a time, making cups of coffee, or lying in bed reading the Sunday papers, or listening to the radio.

When she was thoroughly rested she would put on her oldest slacks and with her head tied in a scarf apply herself to her room, making her bed with clean sheets, sorting her clothes into piles of "clean" (to be hung up), "dirty" (to be washed), and "crumpled" (to be ironed). Then she would dust her furniture and scrub the woodwork, strew the hall with buckets of hot water, dusters, and polishing rags, and have the vacuum roaring merrily for hours. Then, feeling efficient and virtuous, she would have a bath and wash her hair.

In the afternoons, she used to meet Linda at the corner of the West End of Princes Street and they would walk the whole length of the street, looking into all the shop windows deciding what they would buy if only they had the cash. When they were exhausted they would buy ice cream and wander in the Gardens or sit on a seat and watch the passersby and criticize their clothes — the fat old grannies in shapeless coats down to their ankles and the beat brigade with their filthy jeans and peculiar hairdos and the mods in their weird gear; just occasionally they would see someone whom they thought was dressed just right.

They usually met friends from school either walking in pairs or, looking self-conscious, with boys. They would look each other up and down, compare escorts, make fashion notes, and exchange news of what could be bought where. Maura used to go around with a boy called Freddie, but he had now left school and gone south to work, and ever since she had been around with Linda. All the best boys seemed to have left and the ones in her class, she thought, were impossibly silly or conceited, and only interested in motor scooters or jazz. They wore awful clothes and never had enough money to pay a girl's bus fare, let alone take her to the movies, and none of them seemed to know how a girl ought to be treated. Maura definitely preferred older men with proper jobs and decent manners, but with all this exam-cramming a girl's social life was bound to become rather limited.

In the evenings she would have a hurried bout with the remains of her homework, press her school skirt, and check that she had a clean white blouse for Monday morning.

So she had every excuse for not going to the country with the family. Nevertheless Maura knew that her real reason had been connected with her resentment at Dad's behavior.

This Sunday she was glad to have the house to herself without Mum nagging about the untidiness of her room or Dad enquiring tenderly and anxiously about her homework or Caroline's continual questions. The only drawback was that Dad had not had time to go out to buy the Sunday papers. However, Maura had a magazine left over from the day before, so when the family had departed, she made herself a cup of coffee and retired with it to bed. She didn't read serious novels on Sunday mornings.

Then it was time for her bath and shampoo. She put the radio on the hall table and left the bathroom door open so that she could join in the songs. What would it be like to be a famous pop singer, she wondered. She didn't really want to be one but it was fun to dream. *That astonishing slip of a girl, Maura Cafferty, who has become the idol of the teen scene . . . interviewed in her fabulous riverside London flat . . . wearing* (let me see) *a sea-green tunic with gold stockings and slippers and reclining on her white velvet sofa . . . How many proposals has she had? "Oh I lost count ages ago . . . ." Her new record is her third to reach the top of the charts.* She raised her foot, her toes like red cherries from the hot water, and turned on the hot water again.

She scrambled some eggs for lunch, ate an apple and drank another cup of coffee before

46

deciding what to wear. Her green skirt and matching blouse? The skirt had a stain on the front and the blouse was elderly and sagging. Her wool dress was hopelessly old-fashioned. It would have to be her brown jumper and last year's brown paisley-pattern blouse. And whatever she wore, she'd have to cover it with her old green corduroy coat. If only she had a spring suit! And some new shoes! How mean Dad was! After all, it was his duty to see his daughter decently dressed. He ought to enjoy seeing her look nice.

"I look a right mess," she said aloud, studying her reflection in the mirror, but actually she didn't look bad at all. "With her figure she can wear anything," she explained to her unseen audience. She knew it was moronic, but she often talked to herself. Then she gave her hair a last comb through and hurried off to meet Linda.

When they had finished window shopping they decided it was warm enough to sit in Princes Street Gardens if they could find a seat facing the sun. Maura was vaguely conscious that it was a nice day, that the winter grass was green again and that some of the trees showed pink blossom, but she wasn't crazy about gardens like Dad and Caroline; what she was interested in was people.

She settled down for a good gossip with Linda.

"You know what?" Linda said. "I saw Jean out with Peter last night."

"Crikey, do you think she's stopped going around with Richard?"

"I don't know."

"But did they look, you know, as if . . . ?"

"They were in the movie line but not holding hands if that's what you mean by your delicate hesitation."

"But going to the movies together, I mean it's pretty obvious."

"I'm sorry for Richard. He really likes her a lot."

"Personally," said Maura, "I can't see what she sees in him. He's nothing special."

"Oh I dunno," said Linda reflectively. "He has got something."

"Yes, shortbackandsides."

They giggled comfortably. Maura didn't mind people having short hair — or long hair for that matter. It was when people thought it was important that she minded, because neither automatically made you into someone special.

"Look, there's Michael," said Linda, not pointing, but giving a jerk of her head.

"Where?" Michael was a boy in their class, moderately intelligent but nothing to rave about.

"Over there. With a boy I don't know."

Maura looked and saw who she meant.

"Isn't he that boy who left the summer before last?" she said at length.

"Which one?"

"You know, the one who edited the school magazine. Geoff something or other."

"Could be. He's not bad," agreed Linda.

"Ssh, they'll hear us."

The two boys came up. Michael was tall and thin with dark floppy hair and acne scars. His friend Geoff was not as tall, and he had smooth, copper-colored hair, gray-green eyes, and freckles. Maura felt a twinge of curiosity because Geoff had been something of a character at school, carrying off unlikely prizes, for instance, and writing poetry, and he did appear to have poise, not like those awful gangly schoolboys. Nor did he wear jeans or flashy Carnaby Street horrors, just dark straight trousers, a gray turtleneck and an ordinary jacket.

"Hullo, folks!" said Michael.

"Hullo!" said the girls.

"Studying the talent?"

"Talent? I haven't seen any," said Linda.

"Well, there is now. Do you remember Geoff, the famous literary critic and news sleuth?"

So it *was* him. Linda looked up and smiled but Maura tried to look cool and distant.

"Geoff," she said vaguely, as if she were trying to dredge her memory. "I think so."

"I'm glad I'm famous," said Geoff easily.

"What are you doing now?" asked Linda while Maura, eyes cast down, looked bored. She didn't intend by asking questions to make these boys even more conceited than they probably were already. Let them ask her.

"Geoff's a journalist," said Michael proudly, as if some of the prestige belonged to him.

"Hardly a journalist yet," said Geoff modestly. "I'm just a reporter on the *Leith Gazette*. Not for me the thundering editorials about the state of nations. I just write up such notable social events as Old Age Pensioners' tea parties and church bazaars."

Now Maura looked at him directly. He was

conceited all right, and sure of his ability to please, but somehow she didn't mind. In a way it was flattering when someone showed off especially to please you. He smiled as if to imply, "You understand what I'm talking about even if the others don't." She liked that too.

"Is it fun?" she murmured.

"Not much, but you have to have experience before you can land a really good job. Actually I don't think I'll stay with the *Gazette* much longer. I'll move to the *Herald* for a couple of years and then me for Fleet Street. There's not much scope in Scotland."

This was a bit different, Maura thought, someone with ideas and ambitions who was not going to stick to a safe mealticket for the rest of his life like Linda's father (or Dad for that matter).

"How about it, folks, shall I buy you all coffee?" asked Geoff, addressing them all but looking particularly at Maura, "After all, I'm the only earning member of this community."

So they moved off out of the Gardens and across Princes Street to a café. Geoff, with a certain assurance, put his hand under Maura's elbow to guide her across the street, but Michael wandered across, hands in pockets, leaving Linda to fend for herself. Aha, thought Maura, manners!

It was Geoff's party. Avoiding what Maura considered all that "awful schoolboy jargon," he talked about his amusing life as a junior reporter, attending weddings, fires, Tory bazaars, and children's sports days. She knew he was

talking to impress her and it was only by concentrated study of her hands and her handbag,
and watching him when he was not watching
her, that she appeared to remain unimpressed.
He talked about "batting out a piece," "de-
livering copy," "covering a story," about subs
and copy-tasters and pars and rejigs, while under her eyelashes Maura studied his freckles,
his big bony nose, his nicely shaped mouth, and
his hands which reminded her of Dad's, and
listened to his voice which was neither genteel
Edinburgh nor gutter-Scots. She did not talk
much about herself but allowed Linda to make
it clear that she was brainy and going to university in the autumn, and would have a career
instead of disappearing into the dish water.

"What will you do?" he asked, looking at
Maura with those gray-green eyes that were as
clear as glass.

"Teach, probably," said Maura, wishing it
sounded more glamorous.

"Somehow I can't see you as a teacher."

"Think of the lovely long vacations," she replied, though she knew what he meant, or
hoped she knew.

"Think of me in the Civil Service," chipped in
Linda. "I can't imagine myself either but we all
have to grow up, or so they say. No doubt I'll
have my in-tray and my out-tray and my pend-
ing-tray just like all the others, and write dreary
letters full of phrases like 'having regard to the
fact that.' "

"You academic types make me sick," Michael
joined in. "I'm going to be an electrical engi-

51

neer and earn as much as all three of you put together. Electricity's the thing nowadays."

"He's right, you know," said Geoff. "In ten years' time I'll be begging him for an interview and be kept waiting in the outer office with his ten secretaries."

"In the technological revolution electricity has a vital role to play," hammed Michael. "What the country needs is-ah electricity and-ah more electricity if it is to reap the-ah fruits of the-ah technological revolution and-ah —"

"Oh shut up," said Linda.

"My God, I've got to get out a story tonight," Geoff suddenly interrupted. "Can I walk you to your bus, Maura?"

It was the first time he had said her name directly and though she felt as if she'd had a shot of ultraviolet rays, she managed to reply nonchalantly that she usually walked. All the same, she said good-bye to the other two and allowed Geoff to escort her to the bus stop on the other side of Princes Street.

"I don't really have to work tonight. I just wanted a minute alone with you," Geoff said, guiding her elbow.

Maura meant to reply flippantly but she felt so weak and happy and tingling with anticipation that she just smiled stupidly and said, "Did you?" Brilliant!

"You're the most surprising girl," Geoff said. "I'm not usually much of a skirt chaser but now, well, this is different. Couldn't we go and have another cup of coffee by ourselves?"

"I mustn't be late," Maura said automatically, not really caring a fig.

So they passed the bus stop and turned left up Lothian Road. It was dusk and the lamps were shining on the new buds of the trees making them look like — Maura tried to think what they did look like and remembered Shelley's "Swarm of golden bees." Yes, the buds were exactly like a swarm of golden bees. The Castle was opaque against the darkening sky and she felt she loved everything about Edinburgh, the warm lamps, the purring traffic, the brightly lit shops, even the cold spring wind that whipped her skirts.

Geoff put his arm through hers in a proprietory way and squeezed it gently. She felt delicious waves of electricity all over her body.

"Perhaps you're hungry," said Geoff at last, solicitously.

Maura tried to think. The part of her body that usually felt hungry simply didn't seem to exist.

"Not specially."

"Coffee, then. And a sandwich."

So they sat at a wooden table in a small smoky café and drank coffee and talked. The words bubbled out of their mouths, they finished each other's sentences and laughed at identical moments. And it wasn't, thought Maura when she could think, just frivolous small talk; he even liked poetry, for instance. She told him about the golden bees and he said delightedly, "So you actually read poetry?"

"Sometimes," Maura said cautiously.

"But it's so stupidly taught at school," he finished. "Whom do you have? That awful old stick, Gatehouse?"

"Yes, and he's dead dull, always carrying on about clauses."

"Grammar's out of date. It'll all be done by computers soon."

"Hooray. What do you like?"

"Modern stuff mostly; you know, Dylan Thomas and Wallace Stevens and Norman McCaig. I even try to write it myself in weak moments."

"Why weak moments?"

"No future in it. But it's fun. Journalism's the thing nowadays."

"Perhaps you'll be a famous journalist," said Maura and really meant it. It was a distinct possibility, not like her own daydreams of being a pop singer or Dad's crazy schemes.

"I intend to be," Geoff said, absolutely seriously. "I want to travel all over the world, writing about revolutions and things."

"I'd like to travel too," said Maura, thinking of the foreign trips they'd probably never have, "but not where there are revolutions. I'd like —"

"To lie in the sun. I know. I'd like that too. This is an abominable climate."

Maura smiled secretly; the climate wasn't bothering her.

"Do you like jazz?" she asked. She'd better find out as soon as possible because the thought of long sessions over some dreary LP featuring drums might be more than she could put up with.

"Some," said Geoff. "I've got an LP I'd like to play you, with a fabulous trumpet."

"I like pop," Maura said, making it quite clear that jazz trumpets left her cold.

"I do, if it's offbeat. Not the sweet syrupy kind. Maura, when can I see you again? I have to work most evenings but the paper comes out on Thursdays so I have Thursdays off. What would you like to do? Do you like Chinese food?"

"Mmm," she said, never having eaten Chinese food but not liking to admit her ignorance.

"Shall I pick you up at your home?"

"Oh don't bother," she said nervously. She could not bear the thought of introducing him to Dad and Mum, not just yet anyway, and snobbishly she didn't want him to see her ordinary shabby home. She wanted to get to know him slowly and privately without any family complications.

"What about meeting outside the movies then, you know, the Pavilion. Would half-past seven do?"

"Okay," said Maura, relieved and a little ashamed of feeling relieved.

"I wish we didn't have to wait till Thursday. Shall I walk you home now? Where do you live?"

"Newington, just the other side of the Meadows."

"Oh good, I like the Meadows after dark."

He paid for the coffee and the sandwiches, and they stood for a moment outside the café, smiling into each other's eyes.

"That was nice," Geoff said. "Now you must take my arm or you'll trip over a tree root and fall on your pretty nose. I can see in the dark; I have cat's eyes."

They walked very slowly along the path, the same one that Caroline took on her way to school. Now it was shadowed mysteriously with the lamplight lighting up the tree buds again.

"More golden bees," said Geoff, looking up at them.

"And green bees," said Maura.

"There are stars too."

"Silver bees," murmured Maura.

"Can you hear them humming?"

"Silly, that's the wind."

"So it is," said Geoff.

When they reached the far end of the walk Maura stopped in order to say good-bye. She didn't want Dad seeing her out of the window.

"Good-bye, Geoff," she said, though it was the last thing she wanted to say.

"Good-bye," said Geoff.

Then he took both her hands and leaned forward and very gently touched her cheek with his lips.

"Good night, Maura. You're — no, I'll have to go home and look in the dictionary to find the word — if there is one. Good night."

6

Caroline was thrilled at spending a day in the country. For a second a shadow had passed over Daddy's face when she had told him that Maura was not coming, but he recovered almost immediately.

"Never mind," he said gaily. "We'll have a grand day, just the three of us. It'll be a nice change doing a day's work without any damned foreman breathing down my neck."

So on Sunday morning at nine o'clock, when Maura was still asleep, the three of them were looking out of the window, dressed in country clothes, waiting for Professor Giles Oxton's car. When it arrived they hurried downstairs and Daddy introduced them before getting in beside the Professor. Caroline and her mother, who were too shy to say more than "Pleased to meet you" and "Hullo," climbed into the back.

The professor was a thin, gray man with very dark bright eyes and a small mouth shut in by long lines running from nose to chin. He had a round shiny bald patch in the middle of his head and a thin dry voice. He punctuated what he said with rasping chuckles through an almost closed mouth, and a wave of one hand. The back of the car was full of plants for his garden.

Although he was a professor of Greek he appeared to be interested in a great many other things — architecture, for instance, and the state of agriculture in the Borders, how dry stone dikes were built, and Roman remains.

Caroline looked out of the window and exclaimed at the sight of lambs and calves and rivers while Mum sat back listening proudly to clever Daddy asking intelligent questions about architecture, farming, and Roman remains.

It took them about an hour to reach the cottage, which was just outside a small village. It was a prim, square building set back from the road, built in red sandstone with two windows, one on each side of a slated porch, and it was roofed with dull purple slates.

"A very sound example of rural architecture," said the Professor, getting out of the car and squinting up at it with a professional air. "About two hundred years old, I should think, wouldn't you, Mr. Cafferty?"

"I couldn't say. I don't really know much about cottages," Daddy had to admit.

The professor unlocked his front door with a big black key and showed them inside. Caroline was terribly disappointed. She had been expecting a proper cottage with a rocking chair, flowery curtains, a cupboard piled with willow-pattern plates, and a kettle slung over the range on a hook. In fact it was hardly furnished at all; there was just a table, two rather ugly fireside chairs, and a cupboard or two.

"I think we'd better light the fire," said the professor, fussily producing a box of matches. "I always leave it ready laid. And I think we should have some coffee before we start work. Would you," he turned to Caroline, "like to walk up the road to the farm and get a pint of milk? I usually have it put in a lemonade bottle. And I'll explain to Mr. Cafferty about the job. I got the electricity people to bring the wires to the front door and install the meter but the rest is up to us."

Caroline walked slowly up the road. She sniffed the air, which was damp and leafy and fragrant. A white cherry tree leaned over a green hawthorn hedge. In the field were some small white lambs with black faces frisking around their fat stodgy mothers. She listened to the country noises, the wind in the trees, the baa-ing of the lambs, the twitter of birds, and the gurgle of a little stream that ran, buried in grass, by the side of the road. How lovely to live in the country, thought Caroline, to have a cottage and a garden and go every day to fetch the milk. She only hoped that a fierce farm dog would not come bouncing out at her.

The farm seemed curiously deserted, as farms so often do. There were a couple of gray cats sitting in the sun and two enormous geese that looked at her out of flat glassy eyes and made indignant gabbling noises. Caroline could not decide whether she ought to go to the front or to the back door but the presence of the geese decided her. She went up to the front door, rang a bell, and waited.

The woman who answered the door was gray-haired and pink-faced, wearing a dark blue apron and Wellington boots.

"Could I have a pint of milk, please?"

"Surely. Have you got a can?"

"No, I've got a lemonade bottle."

"That'll do fine. Wait a minute, will you?"

The woman took the bottle and disappeared and Caroline wondered if another time she might be allowed to follow her into the cowshed or dairy or wherever she was going. When she came back Caroline thanked her. "Yes," she told her, "we are just down for the day. Daddy is helping Professor Oxton with his electricity and we are going to have a picnic lunch." Then she said good-bye, and set off back down the road feeling highly satisfied with the success of her expedition.

Inside the cottage the fire was burning brightly and her mother had boiled a kettle on the gas stove and put white cups and saucers and a packet of sugar on a tray. Daddy had taken off his jacket and laid his tools handily on the floor. He had found a stepladder and was examining the meter. The professor was standing in front of the fire making a speech.

"Modern civilization frightens me," he was saying, "positively frightens me. If indeed it can be called civilization when we are purposely destroying the very basis of what we mean by civilization — the production of art, the enjoyment of leisure and tranquillity." Amazed, Caroline listened to the spate of words. Apparently airplanes, automobiles, television sets, and newspapers had all been a great mistake and people living in ancient Athens had been much happier in every way.

"What about the slaves?" her father interrupted smartly — he loved an argument.

"I grant you, I grant you," said the professor, waving his arms, "but we have machines to do the work of slaves so we have even less excuse for our degraded existence. We have lost every natural skill we ever possessed. We can't dig or build or carve or play musical instruments. Look at me, the product of an expensive and prolonged education, but have I mastered the first principles of electricity? No. Do I know how and when to plant vegetables in my garden? No. Could I repair the slates on my roof? No."

"Daddy knows all about gardens and electricity," said Caroline proudly, sipping her coffee.

"Your father is a remarkable man, my dear."

"Even if he can't understand Greek," said Daddy, but not as though he minded.

The day passed pleasantly. Caroline and her mother went for a walk; they all had a substantial and messy lunch and Daddy even found time to show the professor how to bed his plants. Caroline watched them: her father, easy and confident, surveying the ground with a professional eye or bending to examine the soil, while the Professor kept pausing in his digging to make speeches about the beneficial effects of manual labor. Caroline supposed that as it was his job to give lectures he had just got into the habit of it.

"Oh it's grand, the open-air life," agreed her father, "but poorly paid."

"Do you have a garden in Edinburgh?"

"No, we do not. I wish we did. But we'll move to the country one of these days, won't we, Caroline?"

"Oh yes, please, Daddy," Caroline agreed fervently.

"I should have thought you could build up a nice little business somewhere like this, Kelso, for instance," said the professor, mopping the round bald patch on his head with a white handkerchief.

"It's like this," her father said confidentially, "I don't like working for a boss so why should folk like working for me?"

"That is indeed a quandary," said the professor, "to boss or to be bossed."

"Now, Caroline," Daddy said, changing the subject, "what about doing some weeding; we can't have you idling about while we work. Do you know which are weeds?"

"I'm not sure."

"Look then, I'll show you. This is chickweed — out. This is dandelion — out. This is grass — out. This is willow herb — definitely out or it'll overrun the whole garden."

"I see," said Caroline, and began grubbing in the cool damp earth.

"And I must stop being foreman and get on with my own job. About power points, Professor, have you made up your mind where you want them?"

"I — er — well, you know I think the best thing would be for you to consult your wife. She'll be the best judge."

"Right," said Daddy, and swung off down the garden whistling, "The Boys of Wexford."

The professor might be able to make speeches, thought Caroline, but he was a very poor digger; he puffed and panted and frequently paused to mop his head or to light a cigarette. Then he looked at his watch and said it was time they were pushing off.

In the car on the way home Daddy, who looked so happy and at ease that he might not have had a care in the world, sang Irish songs, at first under his breath and then, at the Professor's request, aloud. He sang "Galway Bay" and "The Strutters' Ball" and "Kevin Barry" and whenever he stopped Caroline would suggest the name of another. So they were home in no time at all and the professor asked them to come again soon.

"I'll never manage the garden without your expert help," he said. "Thank you all very much."

At home Caroline carefully took off her muddy shoes while Mum hurried into the kitchen to heat a big panful of soup she had made the day before.

"Run and ask Maura if she wants some, will you, Caroline?" she asked.

Caroline tapped on Maura's door but there was no reply. She poked her head in but the room was empty.

"Maura's out," she reported. "She said she was going to tidy her room but it doesn't look as if she has."

"Now, now, don't tell tales," reproved her father. "Do you know where she's gone?"

"Out with Linda, she said."

"Och well, she'll likely have her tea there."

They settled down to their soup, and then Daddy hid himself behind the Sunday paper he had bought on the way home. However, he seemed to be listening for something; he kept commenting on Maura's lateness, and several times he rose to look out of the window as if he hoped to see her walking up the street.

7

After she had said good night to Geoff, Maura ran the last hundred yards home under the singing lamplight. She did not want to see Mum or Dad, she wanted to be alone to remember Geoff's kiss and how he had said, "You're — but I can't think of the word. I shall have to go home and look it up in the dictionary." She wanted to relive every second of their time together. Outside the front door she paused for a moment and shut her eyes so that she could better imagine him: that coppery-colored hair falling in rough yet smooth feathers, those clear greenish eyes like a cat's with the thick fair lashes, the golden freckles on his nose, the way his two eye teeth were slightly crooked, and the nice energetic way he talked. She was glad he hadn't kissed her properly — even that gentle wisp of a kiss was more exciting than any kiss Freddie had ever given her. At last she took a deep breath, inserted her latchkey and open the door.

"Maura, is that you? You're dreadfully late."

"Oh dear," she thought, "oh dear, oh dear, oh dear!"

"Yes it's me, Mum," she said, as she dawdled blinking in the kitchen.

"Where in the world have you been?" Dad asked, nervously and angrily.

"With Linda," she said quickly.

"You know you're supposed to be home early on Sundays."

"Sorry, we were talking," Maura said sulkily. How she loathed stupid explanations. She shouldn't have to explain where she'd been at her age.

"I don't like you coming home alone in the dark," muttered Dad.

"Oh, Dad, for goodness' sake, I'm not a baby. I've come home alone thousands of times."

She couldn't imagine why on earth he should be making such a fuss. Parents were so unpredictable.

"Did you have your tea with Linda? Or will I heat you some soup?" Mum asked soothingly.

"It's all right, I don't want any. I'll go to bed now." All she wanted was to be alone, but Dad persisted.

"You've been with your friends all day and now you haven't a minute to spend with your mother and me. I suppose you don't want to hear what we've been doing."

The thought of having to look interested while Dad told her about his professor and what the country looked like at this time of the year (as if she didn't know), and how clever he'd been with the electricity, filled her with desperate boredom.

"But, Dad, my homework —" she began, but this was a mistake.

"Your homework!" he exploded. "Do you

mean that with all the day to yourself you haven't even managed to finish your homework?"

"There's just something I want to check," she lied.

"She's tired," Mum said placatingly. "We'll tell her about everything tomorrow."

But Dad wasn't in the mood to be placated.

"Starting homework at ten o'clock at night — it's absurd. You'll be half asleep tomorrow."

If he only knew how ridiculous he looked — and sounded, thought Maura. She fidgeted with her feet and wished now that she'd acted the part of his darling daughter. It would have been shorter and pleasanter in the long run to have rushed up to him in the way she used to do and have asked him about his day and told him about hers. Now he was clearly on a fault-finding tack and she could see him searching his mind for something else to pick on. Then he found it.

"Your room's a disgrace. Your mother's had to tidy it for you. You're a lazy, selfish —"

At this Maura lost her temper.

"Oh, Dad, quit nagging," she almost shouted.

"Maura, don't speak to your father like that."

"Good night," she yelled and slammed out of the room.

Passing Caroline's door she heard a sleepy voice calling out, "Maura."

Maura put her head into the room. "You still awake?"

"Mmm."

Maura went in. She rather liked having a bedtime chat with Caroline. "I've had such a super time," she said dreamily.

"What did you do?"

"Sat in the Gardens with Linda and I met —" She stopped herself just in time; it wouldn't be sensible to talk about Geoff even though she was longing to do so. "Oh, I met some friends and we drank coffee and talked."

"What did you talk about?"

"Oh, all sorts of things."

"We had a super day too. The professor's nice but he talks all the time as if he was giving lectures. And he's got a round bald patch."

She paused and then Maura realized why she had really called her in. "Why is Dad cross? I thought he was in a good mood. He sang all the way home."

"He's just being rotten and old-fashioned," Maura said scornfully, "I'm grown up and he goes on treating me as if I were a two-year-old."

This appeared to satisfy Caroline for she changed the subject. "I'd like to live in the country. Dad says we will someday."

"Someday!" Maura repeated contemptuously. "He's been saying that ever since I was born. Anyhow, who wants to live in the stupid old country," she said, remembering the lights and the dark castle and the budding trees and the stars and Geoff's arm in hers. "I think Edinburgh's fabulous."

"I'll live in the country when I'm grown up," said Caroline sleepily, "in a cottage with flowery curtains and a rocking chair, and I'll go every day to fetch the milk in a lemonade bottle."

Maura smiled and gave her sister an affectionate rumple.

"You do that. I'll come and visit you. Good night, Carol."

"Good night."

She tiptoed into her own room and took out her geometry book. She still had a problem to do, but she did not really care if the wretched triangle was isosceles or equilateral or whether the angles were obtuse or acute. She just wanted to think about Geoff. Would he be thinking of her? She hoped so. If only Thursday would hurry up and come!

It came at last, and the Chinese meal was delicious; they giggled over the chopsticks and burned their fingers on the tiny handleless cups.

After that they started meeting the two or three evenings a week that Geoff usually had free. And often they could spend whole Sundays together because Dad had stopped asking her to go with them to the professor's cottage, for which Maura was devoutly thankful. Dad appeared to have taken over the garden as well as the electricity. According to Mum, he and Caroline weeded and dug and planted while the professor strolled about with a trowel in one hand, making speeches about the glories of rural life and the superior values of ancient Greek society, and Mum herself cooked dinner on the antique stove. Maura would have been bored to tears.

Geoff was the energetic outdoor type and to her surprise Maura found that she honestly enjoyed walking along the foreshore at Cramond or on the Pentland Hills quite as much as window shopping. One advantage of such outdoor activities was that she didn't need many new clothes, just cotton skirts and sneakers, though she drew the line at wearing jeans.

However, what she liked best was strolling in the Botanic Gardens, for there were lots of secluded spots there where they could kiss without being gaped at. Geoff would read out the funny Latin names on the trees and shrubs. And he would take her to the modern art gallery where they would giggle at the queer pictures, all blobs and squiggles, and then have coffee at one of the rickety tables outside.

On wet days they used either to sit in cafés drinking innumerable cups of coffee or go to Geoff's house and sit in a happy daze, playing records or *not* watching television. At first she had been alarmed at the prospect of meeting Geoff's parents, but they turned out to be quite dull and innocuous.

His father was a government clerk in St. Andrews House, a "silver" servant as Linda called it, and he never said much to her except "Hullo" and "How's Maura today?" She would smile and say, "Fine, thanks, Mr. Collingwood," and that was that. Geoff's mother was one of those fusspots who think that no one can be happy unless he is continuously eating and drinking. So while they sat in Geoff's room, which was crowded with books and magazines and records, she would tap nervously at the door, offering them coffee, tea, Coca-Cola, biscuits, sandwiches, and cake. Both his parents seemed to be rather in awe of Geoff, who treated them kindly and patronizingly, as if they were devoted family retainers.

"They're quite nice," Geoff said generously, "but hopelessly illiterate. They just haven't a clue about anything. How about yours?"

"They're all right," Maura said vaguely. Somehow it was difficult to describe Dad, his showing off and his fake Irish accent and the way he turned everything that happened to him into high drama, not to speak of his embarrassing way of bursting into song.

"Dad's parents were Irish," she said at last, "so he has to be Irish too. And he's always singing those awful folk songs."

"The Bonny Lass of Ballochmyle" and all that?"

"And setting old Ireland free."

"Aha, a patriot."

"Yes, his father took part in the Easter Rising and he goes on and on about it."

"What's your mother like?"

"She's nice but she's had an awful life; Dad's always walking out of jobs." Maura paused. She suddenly had a vivid picture of Mum's blissful face as she murmured, "Dennis, oh, Dennis." "They both seem quite fond of each other," she added hastily. "The trouble is that they will treat me as if I was about five."

"That, my darling, is a constitutional defect in all parents," Geoff said. "They can't bear to realize that their fledglings are old enough to fly away from the nest. I've had to be firm with mine or they'd still be fussing whether I'd had a proper dinner or was wearing my winter woolies. Still, I have them pretty well under control."

"Lucky you," Maura said enviously.

"Not lucky, sensible. Still, I'd better come

and inspect yours some time. You're not keeping me a deathly secret are you?"

"Of course not!" Maura lied swiftly, because this was exactly what she had been doing.

"In these situations," Geoff went on, "I think it's best to break them in gently, let them get used to the idea."

Maura badly wanted to ask him to expand on the words "situation" and "idea," but she decided to be noncommittal. "You're probably right," she said.

She wasn't quite sure why she had such aversion to allowing Geoff to call for her or to bring her home. Time after time she had imagined conversations in which she said casually, "Oh, Dad, this is Geoff; he's taking me to the movies," or "Can I bring a friend home to tea? — his name's Geoff — he seems quite nice," but at the last minute she had always panicked. She wanted to produce exactly the right casual note in her voice; yet she had a horrid feeling that she was more likely to blush or stammer, and everyone knew how psychological it was to stammer over a person's name. It was absurd. She'd brought home boys before — Freddie had come around quite often — and both Dad and Mum had behaved perfectly adequately, not drowning him with questions or freezing him with suspicious silence as some parents did. But Geoff was quite different from Freddie; they were really in love and she could not bear anything to be spoiled. It mattered to her more than she cared to admit that Dad and Geoff should like each other.

So she always said she was going for a walk with Linda or having tea with her so that they could do their homework together or that there was a meeting of the Literary Society at school. And all the time she knew that these were stupid, unnecessary lies and that the longer she left it the harder it would be to introduce Geoff with offhand confidence.

Things were going rather well at home. Dad was working in a small engineering shop in Leith, making radio parts or something, and he bought Maura her new shoes almost immediately. His Sundays in the country kept him in a good temper and Maura took particular care to ask the right questions and to listen to the answers. So it seemed a pity to risk disturbing the peace since he might so easily take a violent dislike to Geoff; Dad would be bound to notice that they were in love and would probably say she was too young or something stupid.

Still Geoff must have been thinking it rather odd, so at length she told him he could call for her the following Sunday and meet the family. Actually it was a bit of a cheat because although they weren't going to the cottage Maura felt pretty certain that they'd be off somewhere visiting some ancient monument. Still, there was always a chance that they could change their minds.

But they didn't, and somewhat relieved Maura lay snugly and sleepily in bed listening to them preparing for an expedition to Roslyn Chapel. Caroline was yelling that she'd lost a shoe, Dad was shaving in the bathroom and singing "The

73

Minstrel Boy to the War Has Gone," and Mum was insisting that sweaters and raincoats be taken "just in case." They shouted good-bye, the front door clicked, and Maura was alone. She heaved a sigh of pleasure. She had done the right thing but now she would not have to take the consequences, and Geoff could remain her own secret. She had plenty of time to bathe, to wash her hair, tidy the house, and make sandwiches for a picnic lunch.

When she looked out of the window, however, she saw that it was raining, not a whimsical little shower, but that steady sort of downpour that meant rain for the rest of the day. How maddening! she thought, and then, how gorgeous! I'll cook dinner for Geoff and show him what being married to me will be like.

Up till now they had been too happy to discuss the future. In fact sometimes Maura had felt a little left out when Geoff began holding forth about being a foreign correspondent and traveling all over the world. She wasn't sure where she came in. She could easily imagine herself as the wife of a famous journalist but she hadn't considered the practical details of the intermediate stages. At some point, obviously, they would get married, but so far Geoff had not mentioned it. Lying in the bathtub Maura thought about being married to Geoff. She would be exquisitely dressed, acting as hostess to his distinguished friends, greeting him when he returned home from some exhausting mission, unobtrusively drawing from the oven his favorite dish, telling interviewers what it felt like to be married to a famous journalist. *Mrs. Geoffrey Collingwood, immaculate in a dark linen suit, was preparing lunch for ten when I visited her in her converted Sussex farmhouse. . . . How to be a good hostess? I've no idea. I just know that Geoff always likes to bring his friends home, and I give them something simple, a rice dish perhaps or steak and lots of salad and fruit. Oh yes, he always discusses his ideas with me and often takes my advice; I give him the woman's angle, you see. And wherever he is, Hong Kong or Athens or Moscow or New York, he always phones me on my birthday and on our wedding anniversary. My recipe for a happy marriage? I just know I love him and he loves me.*

"I love him and he loves me," she sang, stepping out of the bath, remembering the poem Geoff had read the other night:

My true love hath my heart and I have his,
By just exchange one for another given;
I hold his dear and mine he cannot miss,
There never was a better bargain driven.
My true love hath my heart and I have his.

How lucky she was that Geoff was not one of those brusque, reticent Scots who were afraid to show their feelings in case they were accused of being sentimental.

In the kitchen she encountered a snag in preparing "something simple." She didn't know how to cook rice and there wasn't any steak. But she absolutely refused to open a can of baked beans or to fry eggs and bacon. She examined the refrigerator, on which Dad had just made a down payment. It contained nothing but a lettuce, a piece of cucumber, and half a pound of chopped meat. Dinner would have to be a hamburger steak with an egg on top, a green salad, and a can of fruit. She had a recipe for hamburgers in one of her magazines, so she peeled an onion and chopped it laboriously, sniffling as the fumes made her eyes water, and beat it into the meat. Then she washed the lettuce and sliced the cucumber as finely as possible. She laid the table with side plates and butter knives. This is what marriage will be like, she thought happily, but *I* shall have nice modern cutlery and table mats and straight Swedish glasses and potted plants and pine-paneled walls and a polished cedarwood table and spindleback chairs when *I'm* married.

When the bell rang she let Geoff in, feeling strangely shy.

"Where are they?" he whispered after he had kissed her.

"The parents? Oh, they went out."

"You might have told me," Geoff grumbled. "I've been preparing merry quips and profound observations all morning in order to impress them."

"But I didn't know," said Maura defensively. "They just decided this morning. Dad's on one of his improvement jags."

"Raising the cultural level of the family? I must say I rather like the sound of your Dad. Well, what shall we do? It's lousy weather."

"I thought I'd cook you some dinner."

"Rah rah, Cafferty, an excellent notion."

So Geoff sat in Dad's chair and looked at the paper, while Maura cooked the dinner. She felt a little self-conscious as she lit the gas and started to fry the hamburgers. She kept stealing a look at Geoff from under her eyelashes to see how he was reacting to the domestic scene. However, he seemed quite unconscious of anything unusual and merely read her bits out of the paper, criticizing the style of various inferior journalists and describing how he would have written the articles himself.

"Come and get it," Maura said at last.

"Good-oh, I'm a one as likes my grub."

"I hope you'll like this," Maura said primly.

"I hope so too."

"Can you cook?" she asked when they'd finished.

"Not me, my Mum doesn't allow males in her kitchen. But I'm quite a hand at cleaning up so long as I'm not forced to wear an apron."

"You sit still," said Maura proudly. "This is *my* kitchen."

Geoff, however, insisted and just used it as an excuse to put his arm around her and kiss the back of her neck. Then he returned to Dad's chair and made her sit on his knee. It was lovely though not specially comfortable.

"I looked up some more words in the dictionary," he said between kisses, "words beginning with 'e' — elegant, enticing, entrancing, electrical, and of course essential."

Maura giggled. She loved Geoff to talk nonsense.

"Now, I've just thought of another, efficient. I never guessed you'd be efficient."

He kissed her again, a long warm tender kiss, and she shut her eyes and forgot that one arm was crushed against the back of the chair. She felt as if she were floating in a wonderful glowing sunlit pool with the sun getting hotter and brighter every minute.

At that moment the door opened and Dad, followed by Mum and Caroline, walked into the kitchen.

8

Caroline was miserable; the family expedition to Roslyn Chapel had been a dismal failure because of the rain. They had eaten their picnic lunch early, huddled in raincoats under some trees, and had then decided to take the first bus home. The Chapel, moreover, had been closed to the public because of the Sunday service.

Mum kept saying that she knew it had been going to rain anyway and that she wished she had stayed at home to clean out the kitchen cupboards. Daddy kept saying that if he'd known people were going to be put off from improving their minds by a little rain he would never have volunteered to take them to this famous building. Mum pointed out nastily that the Chapel was closed anyhow. Caroline complained that she was cold because she had forgotten her sweater, and she in turn was scolded for having forgotten it despite her mother's specific reminder. Consequently they had all sat glowering at each other in the bus, while Caroline planned to have a hot bath the moment she got home, put on her warmest robe and her woolly slippers, and sit close to the kitchen fire drinking scalding tea and eating hot buttered toast.

When Daddy opened the kitchen door Caroline, following close behind, saw Maura jumping hastily to her feet, her face pink with embarrassment and her hair tousled. And a young man Caroline had never seen before was also jumping to his feet and smoothing his reddish hair with a quick nervous hand. The house was usually empty when they got back from their expeditions. Now not only were there people here but people involved in mysterious activities of their own. She was surprised, curious, and a little bit alarmed.

"And what's going on here?" burst out Daddy, and Caroline's heart sank. He was going to be even crosser than he had been on the bus.

"This is Geoff," mumbled Maura limply. "He came to take me for a walk, but the rain . . ." Her voice trailed off.

"I'm so glad you've come back," said the strange young man whose name was Geoff. "I've been looking forward to meeting you."

He smiled but Caroline saw that he was also embarrassed. Why? He shook hands with Mum and Daddy. "Hullo, so you're Caroline," he said, smiling at her.

Caroline just stared.

Daddy looked as though he would sooner knock Geoff down than shake hands with him. Instead he vented his anger on Maura.

"So this is why you never want to come out with us," he said furiously; "smuggling young men in as soon as our backs are turned." Caroline got lost in the spate of words and only caught odd phrases, "To think that a daughter of mine — how long has this sort of thing been going on? — disgraceful!"

"Dad!" Maura kept expostulating in an agony of embarrassment.

"But Maura invited me round to meet you," said Geoff, sounding honestly surprised. "She told me . . ." and then his sentence died away. He looked at Maura, seemed to be upset by what he saw, and stared silently at his feet. He had nice suede shoes with elastic sides, Caroline noticed.

"I come home unexpectedly and find my daughter necking in an armchair with a complete stranger," went on Daddy dramatically, glaring at them both.

What did necking mean, wondered Caroline, and why was it wicked?

"Let's have some tea," Mum said soothingly, "and Maura will explain."

Caroline thought longingly of tea but Daddy ignored the suggestion.

"Explain! This'll take some explaining."

"Perhaps I'd better go," said Geoff awkwardly.

"Perhaps you had. My daughter's always been free to bring her friends home. She doesn't have to sneak off and meet them on the sly. If you wanted to see her you should have called round in an open and respectable manner."

"But that's what I've been wanting . . ." and again Geoff looked at Maura and broke off. He tried to smile and started again, "But I *have* called in an open and respectable manner. I didn't know you wouldn't be in."

"I was going to tell you," said Maura, looking as though she were going to cry, "but then you went out."

Caroline wanted to cry too. She couldn't bear

people being angry and shouting at each other. Daddy wasn't like Daddy when he was angry; his eyes narrowed and shone with a peculiar glitter and his mouth reminded her of an animal snarling. And Mum seemed somehow limp and defenseless and frightened. She felt sobs rising in her throat; she rushed over to her mother and gripped her hand tightly.

"There, there," said Mum gently.

"Now you've upset your little sister," said Daddy unfairly, for it wasn't only Maura who had upset her.

"I'll go," said Geoff again. "I'm sorry." He gave Maura a reproachful glance and put on his jacket.

"You can go away and stay away," snapped Daddy; "I know what my responsibilities are. I know how to look after my daughter."

"Bye, Maura," said Geoff tonelessly and went.

Maura burst into a storm of tears and Caroline could bear it no longer. She dashed out of the room, hearing as she ran to her room Maura saying between sobs, "You're unfair and beastly and horrible. Geoff wanted to meet you. It's true! And now you've spoiled everything. He'll never speak to me again. I'm so ashamed."

"So I should hope," retorted Daddy.

Caroline sat on her bed. She wanted to put her fingers in her ears and yet at the same time she wanted to hear everything. She heard Mum's voice, "They're so young, Dennis. I'm sure they didn't meant to do wrong. Maura will say she's sorry and that it won't happen again. Young folks like to be together. They were just thoughtless."

And then more rumbles from Daddy and more reproaches from Maura and more pleading from Mum, and then Maura shouting fiercely, "But I'm not sorry, I'm not sorry at all. Dad's the one who should be sorry, making a fool of me in front of my friend, my very best friend." And then she too ran out of the room.

When she saw Caroline she sat down beside her and put her arms around her. "Don't pay any attention. It's nothing to do with you."

"I don't like it when people shout," sniffled Caroline.

"Neither do I."

They both listened to the voices next door, Daddy's angry and strident, Mum's low and apologetic.

"You're shivering, Caroline."

"I'm cold."

Maura wrapped her in her quilt and tried to comfort her.

"Geoff's so marvelous," she said. "He's a journalist. He's frightfully clever."

"Is he your real boyfriend?"

"Mmm."

"Will I like him?" asked Caroline doubtfully.

"Of course."

"Are you going to get married to him?"

"I expect so."

"Why is Daddy so cross?"

"He's impossible and prehistoric. He just doesn't understand."

"What'll happen now?"

"Oh, it'll all blow over," Maura said unconvincingly. "You know Dad. Tomorrow he'll be asking Geoff to tea and singing 'Kevin Barry' to him."

They both giggled a little hysterically.

"If I couldn't see Geoff again I'd — I'd jump off the Dean Bridge," said Maura dramatically, feeling it was now her turn to be comforted.

"Would you really?" Caroline was awestruck; imagine her own sister, jumping off the Dean Bridge. It was a huge bridge and she had to be lifted up to be able to see the bright tumbling river, the Water of Leith, at the bottom of the almost bottomless gulf.

"I couldn't live without Geoff," Maura said fiercely. "When we get married you can come and stay with us, Carol."

Caroline considererd. "Will you live in the country?"

"Perhaps."

"I'll see," said Caroline judiciously.

"You're just nuts about the country."

The country reminded Caroline of Daddy. "I wish he'd stop being angry," she muttered.

"Well I'm furious with him too," said Maura. "Now I'm going to write to Geoff. And you'd better go down and have some tea. I cooked Geoff's dinner for him and he thought I was a super-efficient cook."

"It's been a horrid day," said Caroline, "and I don't want any tea."

But presently Mum came in with some tea and she allowed herself to be babied and tucked up in bed and kissed good night.

The next few days the house was an uncomfortable place to live in. Caroline was always hearing angry or pleading voices which stopped abruptly when she came into the room, and there would be Maura, looking aggrieved or tearstained, shouting, "Well, I think it's ridiculous; after all I'm almost eighteen," or Daddy saying, "Women shouldn't go out to work and neglect their children. This would never have happened if —" or Mum saying, "The child's unhappy, Dennis, don't you think it would be better if —"; and then they would turn to Caroline with false smiles to ask, "How was school today?" having left their sentences malevolently suspended in midair. Caroline hadn't the heart to reply more than "fine" or "awful." She stopped describing her horrible lunches, what the teacher had said, how Elspeth had a new puppy, and which boy had been punished.

It was only nice when she was alone with one member of the family. Then Maura would tell her how marvelous and mature and ambitious and well-read Geoff was; and how she was going to see him on Thursday if she had to walk over broken bottles; Mum would tell her amusing stories about what happened at the café, how one of her regular customers had had a new baby and brought it in to be admired, and how the girl from a nearby office came in with a different boyfriend every day. Daddy took her on his knee as usual, called her his best girl and described how he had scored off the foreman in an argument about the tea break; or they discussed together the progress of the professor's garden.

The most exciting news was that the professor was going abroad in the summer and had suggested that the Caffertys take over the cottage in his absence. Daddy described in loving detail all the things they would do — walks, picnics, fishing, photography, collecting wild flowers, and gardening. "He'll not recognize his garden when he comes back!" chuckled Daddy. "You and I will work like beavers, Caroline." "Oh yes, Daddy," Caroline would reply eagerly, but at the back of her mind she wondered what would happen to Maura. Maura's idea of a vacation was not staying in a country cottage, gardening, especially if it meant being separated from wonderful Geoff; and if she was forced to come she would probably sulk and spoil everything.

At the same time Caroline allowed herself to become involved in all Daddy's exciting plans. He would find a pony for her to ride, or failing that, a bicycle; they would go out early in the morning and catch fine, fat trout for breakfast; they would have lettuce for tea, fresh from the garden; they would burn logs on chilly evenings and sit around the fire, playing cards or reading aloud. And one of these days they would find a cottage of their own, like the professor's but much nicer, and live there all the year round, getting brown as berries in summer and being snowed up for weeks at a time in winter. But whenever they were cozily chatting, miles away from home, Maura would come in, give Daddy a disdainful look as if to say "You can't fool me, I don't believe a word of it," and Daddy would shut up abruptly.

Mealtimes were the worst because everything everybody said seemed to have another sinister meaning. If Mum talked about her work she seemed to be implying, "I'm going out to work whether you like it or not," and if Daddy praised Caroline he seemed to be hinting that his other daughter was not so satisfactory, and over all their most innocent conversations hung the cold wounded dignity of Maura.

Edinburgh was full of sunshine and beech leaves and gusts of cheerful wind, girls in summer dresses and babies in carriages, and Caroline walked to school nearly every day. Often she wished she could go into the Grassmarket at dawn and jump on the back of a unicorn and gallop away into fairyland where no one was ever cross or miserable.

9

Maura was determined to meet Geoff on Thursday, even if it meant leaving home forever.

She had written to Geoff; it was a very difficult letter to write because what she wanted to say was "Darling Geoff, I'll die if I don't see you again, I'll jump off the Dean Bridge. Please say you still love me and want to marry me, and please forgive me for being so stupid," but this was not the sort of letter that any self-respecting girl could write.

So what she really wrote was:

Darling Geoff,

The parental wrath fell on me, WHAM, CLONK. Honestly, aren't fathers peculiar? I wish I'd trained mine the way you have yours. But mine still appears to have prehistoric notions about the purity of his daughter. Hey nonny nonny no.

It was even more difficult to explain why she had been keeping him a secret, because it must have appeared that either she was ashamed of him or ashamed of her parents, and neither was at all true.

Of course it might have been better to have

Come Clean and said, "Father, I love that man. May he pay his addresses to me?" But for all I know, this might equally have aroused his ire.

Then she crossed out *pay his addresses* and substituted *may he come and call.*

I fear he is the victim of a typical parental neurosis and I'm only sorry you should have borne the brunt of it.

I have no intention of buckling under the iron rod of discipline (buckle, buckle, buckle) and no doubt the storm will blow over, but in the meantime my spirits are somewhat dejected. However my sentiments toward you remain as per usual and always.

Much, much, very, very, love,

Maura

PS. I'll meet you on Thursday as usual outside the theater. Unless I am locked in my chamber . . . does this sort of thing still happen in our enlightened days?

Maura felt quite proud of this effort, which seemed dignified without being cold, and apologetic without being groveling. But Geoff did not reply and by Thursday she was feeling quite desperate. She could not eat any tea and she was terrified Mum would start fussing. She knew if she said she was going to meet Linda no one would believe her. However, as it turned out Dad was going to a trade union meeting, and she simply walked out of the house without saying anything to anyone, but giving Caroline a conniving wink.

She hurried to the theater and was at least ten minutes too early, so she looked at the stills without even noticing the title of the picture and for once she didn't try to catch her reflection in the glass shopfronts. Geoff, Geoff, Geoff, she thought, willing him to appear and sweep her into his arms and tell her that he loved her and that everything would be all right.

But when he did appear it wasn't like that at all. He just said, "Hullo, Maura, I got your letter," and stood looking at her as if she were a thousand miles away. All the things she had meant to say stuck in her throat.

"Hullo," she said limply.

"What's new?"

"Nothing, really."

He didn't smile or touch her hand, and his face was wooden and glum. He just gave a jerk with his head and said still in the same faraway voice, "Come on, we'll walk."

She didn't even dare take his arm as they turned back toward the Meadows and along the same path they had walked together that first evening. She looked up and saw that the beech leaves that had once been golden bees were now transparent green butterflies, but she didn't have the heart to say so.

At last Geoff burst out angrily, "How could you be so stupid? I can't stand people who tell such stupid lies."

"I'm sorry, Geoff," Maura stammered.

"I daresay, but you put me in an intolerable position. And it was all so unnecessary. What's wrong with me anyhow?"

"It wasn't that."

"Why, then, why?"

"I didn't want to spoil anything."

"You've spoiled it now."

"I didn't want to have Dad inspecting you."
He shrugged his shoulders impatiently.

"What are we going to do, Geoff?" she asked
in a small voice. She hoped he would say "Elope
with me," or "Let's get married secretly," or
something utterly drastic and final, but all he
said was, "Do? Call it a day, I suppose. I'm not
going to skulk around meeting you in secret. It's
too ignominious. I'm not a leper."

"You mean, not see each other anymore?" She
could hardly bring the words out.

"Unless you can smooth the old boy down and
put me in the clear — by telling him the truth,
for instance."

"Oh, I couldn't."

"You've turned something perfectly straight-
forward into a silly Victorian melodrama. Life's
complicated enough as it is without inventing
complications."

Maura stared at him in amazed disbelief. This
couldn't be Geoff, the same person who had
called her entrancing and enticing and essential.
He was walking, his hands in his pockets, his
freckled face expressionless, his green eyes fixed
on the ground. He was a complete stranger.

She gave a sort of choked noise and began to
run across the grass because sobs were boiling
up inside her and she simply mustn't cry in
front of this stranger. "I shall die, I shall die,"
she whispered in between sobs. "How can he be

so cruel?" She ran until she was out of breath and then she threw herself onto the grass and put her arms over her head to hide her face and her tears. She wished she were on the Dean Bridge but somehow to get up and wait for a bus to take her there would have been impossible; besides she hadn't even fourpence for the fare. She thought of Keats's "To cease upon the midnight with no pain" and it seemed all wrong that one could not do beautiful dramatic things without waiting for buses and remembering bus money.

She began to cry harder than ever as she imagined herself on the ledge of the Dean Bridge, poised to jump, and thought how sorry Geoff and Dad would be, who between them had driven her to her death. She did not hear Geoff's running footsteps until suddenly he was beside her, and his arms were around her and he was kissing her wet face and babbling, "Maura, darling, I'm sorry. Don't cry. I must have been mad, you know I love you, I didn't mean to hurt you, I'll never give you up."

"Oh, Geoff, I love you so much!" she gulped.

"Don't cry, there's a good girl."

But it was wonderful and comforting to cry with her face pressed against Geoff's shirt and to feel his hands smoothing her hair. When, however, she remembered how ghastly she must look she broke away and sat up.

"I must look a sight. Lend me your hankie."

"You look like a little drowned pussycat," Geoff said tenderly, scrubbing her face with his handkerchief.

She borrowed his comb and combed her hair.

"Now you look like a mermaid."

Maura giggled. "You're not angry with me any longer?"

"I'm furious, but we'll sort it out. When you ran off like that I felt desperate. You're never to do it again."

"Oh I won't, I won't."

And they kissed again.

She felt the smooth skin of his face and the rough feathers of his hair and his hard warm arms pressing her close. Suddenly she shivered and Geoff pulled her to her feet.

"Come on. We'll have some coffee and discuss the plan of campaign."

"I'll talk to Mum," Maura said. "She'll coax Dad around."

"I'll come and talk to him myself. We'll tell him we're engaged. Are we engaged?"

"Oh yes," she breathed rapturously.

"I haven't told you, by the way, but I've got a new job, on the *Herald*. Geoff Collingwood is on his way to that nice room at the top."

"Oh, Geoff, how marvelous."

"Next thing I'll be in Fleet Street."

When Maura got home she was so dizzy with happiness and relief that when she saw Dad sitting in his chair it seemed perfectly easy to go up to him and say, "Dad, I'm sorry. I was a perfect fool."

He looked at her and his face which had been sad and withdrawn became quick and eager, and his eyes which had been cold and stony shone warm and golden again. He hugged her.

"My foolish lassie. Now tell your old Dad all about it."

Mum was smiling too, and she got up and fetched Maura a cup of tea as she sat on the floor at Dad's feet and told him.

"It wasn't Geoff's fault at all," she explained, "it was absolutely mine. I just felt shy. You see I do like him so awfully."

"Am I such an ogre?" asked Dad with raised eyebrows, "or are you ashamed of us?"

"Oh, Dad, of course not. It wasn't that at all. It was just—" But it was too difficult to explain her confused feelings so she went on, "I know you'll like Geoff, he's just got a new job on the *Herald*, he's terribly clever and he's always wanted to meet you, he likes the sound of you."

"Does he indeed?"

"Can he come round on Sunday, to tea?"

"If your mother agrees, yes. I'll give way gracefully," Dad said with a smile. "I'm not one to part young lovers."

"I saw him this evening," Maura said, determined to be completely honest. "He was very angry with me."

She felt Dad's knee stiffen but he only said, "He had every right to be. But he's got to treat my daughter right or I'll break every bone in his body."

"Dad, no."

Just then Caroline, who had been having a bath, came into the kitchen in her bathrobe. She looked at the three of them and her face broke into a grin and she did a little hop-skip as she always did when she was especially pleased.

94

"Ooooh, tea," she said. "Can I have some?"

"Geoff's coming to tea on Sunday," Maura told her.

"Goodie, I like Geoff," said Caroline. She climbed onto Dad's knee and gave him little butterfly kisses on his cheek.

"It's far too late for a wee girl like you to be sitting up drinking tea," Mum said, fondly passing her a cup.

"And how do you know you like Geoff?" asked Dad.

"I just know. He's got green eyes like a cat. And freckles. I've got freckles."

"You'll all like him," Maura said happily.

10

Caroline was excited about Sunday tea and kept asking, "What time will Geoff come?" and "Has Geoff got any little sisters?" and "What's Geoff's other name?" She put on her new pink cotton dress and clean white socks which she had washed the night before.

Mum also seemed excited and nervous. She wanted to have tea in the front room with her best cloth and napkins on the table, but Daddy put his foot down.

"The lad must take us as he finds us, Nora," he protested. "He's not to be treated like royalty. We're eating in the kitchen as usual."

Caroline was disappointed.

Then Mum started fussing about what they were to eat. Maura had told her about all the nice things Geoff's mother had given her and Mum didn't want to be outdone. She baked cakes and scones and asked Maura at intervals, "Does Geoff like chocolate cake? Does Geoff like strawberry jam?" until Maura snapped back, "He likes everything. Don't fuss, Mum. He hates being fussed over."

Even so Mum scrubbed and polished the kitchen floor, enlisting Caroline's help in removing all the newspapers, gloves, scarves, old letters, balls of string, knitting needles, and empty jam jars from their usual cluttered position on the countertop, and persuaded Caroline to polish the cutlery.

Maura herself changed her dress about half a dozen times, shut herself into the bathroom for at least an hour, and kept going to the mirror in the hall to brush her hair and into the kitchen to polish her shoes.

"Suppose you look out of the window and tell us when Geoff's coming," she suggested to Caroline.

When he did arrive it was all rather disappointing. Everyone smiled and shook hands, and Mum spoke in the polite voice she reserved for schoolteachers and ministers. Daddy offered Geoff a cigarette and they all sat down and said what a wonderful day it was except for the east wind, of course, but that was just Edinburgh wasn't it? Meanwhile Caroline examined Geoff with silent concentration — he wasn't anything like so remarkable as the Geoff of her imagination. She wanted him to say something special to her but he just smoked and looked out of the window while Maura fidgeted and gazed at Geoff and Daddy looked abstracted.

"What's being a journalist?" asked Caroline at last.

"Writing bits for newspapers," said Geoff, smiling with relief. "Have you got a copy of yesterday's *Herald?* I'll show you something I wrote."

Caroline rummaged in the closet to which the newspapers had been banished and found a copy.

"There," said Geoff. *"Widow fined for shop-lifting."*

Caroline stared at the little black paragraph and then back at Geoff's face, trying to connect them.

"What's shoplifting?" she asked.

"Stealing things from shops."

"What did she steal?"

"Read it and see."

Widow Mrs. Eileen Tarvet was fined £5 at Edinburgh Magistrates Court yesterday for removing a teddy bear from an Edinburgh department store. Mrs. Tarvet admitted her guilt but explained that the toy was for her grandson's birthday, read Caroline. "Did you write all that?"

" 'Fraid so."

"Why isn't your name on it?"

"I'm not important enough to get a byline."

"What's a byline?"

"My name at the top."

"Do you think the grandson was allowed to keep the teddy bear?"

"That I don't know."

Daddy began to perk up. He loved learning about other people's jobs, and he quickly subjected Geoff to a rapid fire of questions. So Geoff explained how newspapers were written, about reporters and subeditors and copy-tasters and news editors and feature writers and how headlines were chosen.

"Gosh," said Caroline at intervals.

"I could take you over the *Herald* if you liked," Geoff suggested.

"Could I come too?" she demanded.

"Of course."

"Shall we, Daddy?"

"Surely, if Geoff can arrange it. Are you in your union, Geoff, by the way?" Daddy asked suspiciously.

"Of course, we have a closed shop," said Geoff, taking out his National Union of Journalists card and showing it to Daddy. Then they had a long discussion comparing journalists' rules and regulations with electricians' rules and regulations. Caroline did not listen; she just watched, and Maura watched, too, with a proud little smile on her lips.

Trade unions naturally led to politics and so Geoff listened respectfully while Daddy talked about Ireland and they agreed about the spinelessness of the Scots.

"Scotland hasn't fought for her independence since the Battle of Bannockburn," said Daddy contemptuously. "You'll never win independence without a fight."

"I think the days of small nations are over," argued Geoff. "I'm an internationalist. I don't want to be stuck in Scotland all my life."

"You can't have internationalism without nationalism," retorted Daddy. "Independence must come first."

They went on arguing and Caroline, bored, went into the kitchen to help Mum prepare tea. And they were still arguing when she came shyly into the room to announce that it was ready.

She hoped they would not go on talking about trade unions and Ireland and Scotland over tea, and they didn't. Conversation suddenly dried up, and after Geoff had dutifully praised the chocolate cake, there didn't seem anything else to say. Caroline, who had been expecting a more festive atmosphere, was disappointed, and decided to make them talk about something interesting for a change.

"When you and Maura get married can I be a bridesmaid?" she asked.

The reaction astonished her.

Geoff choked on his tea, Maura blushed, Mum gasped, and Daddy looked like a thundercloud. Geoff was the first to recover.

"It's a bit too soon to say. You see we're not really engaged yet."

"Caroline, you're the limit," muttered Maura.

"Caroline, get on with your tea and don't talk about things you don't understand," said Mum sharply.

Caroline blushed. She realized that she had said something awful though she wasn't quite sure why. She did so want to be a bridesmaid. It meant getting a new dress and having a huge tea with lots and lots of lemonade. And Maura *had* said she was going to marry Geoff.

"I should think not," said Daddy fiercely. "Engaged indeed! You're both far too young. Caroline, if you ask all the young men Maura brings to the house when they're going to marry her you'll be most unpopular."

"But — " Caroline began and then thought better of it. Quickly she took another piece of chocolate cake.

"But since the subject's come up," said Geoff

bravely. "Maura and I would like to be engaged."

"I never heard such nonsense!" Daddy said.

"But it's not nonsense, Dad. Lots of girls even get married at seventeen, and I'm almost eighteen."

"Just because there are lots of silly fools about doesn't mean that my daughter has to be one of them," barked Daddy.

Caroline was aghast. Everything had been going so well and the sudden change was all her fault. She looked pleadingly at her mother.

"Let's discuss it some other time," Mum said with a false smile. "More tea, Geoff?"

"We're not going to discuss it at all," thundered Daddy. "Maura's only finishing school at the end of the month and then she's going to university. I'm not going to allow her to ruin her chances with silly ideas of getting engaged and married. She must keep her mind on her work."

Out of the corner of her eye Caroline noticed Maura and Geoff exchanging glances and the very faintest shrugs of their shoulders as if they were saying, "Why must parents be so old-fashioned and peculiar?" Daddy must have noticed it too because he grew even angrier.

"Having boyfriends is one thing — every pretty girl deserves a boyfriend or two — but getting engaged at seventeen! I never heard of anything so ridiculous."

By now Maura had become angry too. "You can't stop us," she cried.

Geoff made another attempt to smooth things

over. "We didn't mean a formal engagement. Just a private understanding. It seemed only fair to tell you."

"You've no business going around asking girls of Maura's age to marry you! Why, you're not even twenty-one yourself."

"As long as they're prepared to wait —" began Mum.

"Prepared to wait? Of course they've got to wait. That's why it's so absurd. Maura ought to be free for years yet before she makes up her mind. Marriage is a serious business."

Now it was Mum's turn to get angry. Nine times out of ten she would agree with Daddy but the tenth time she could shout, just as he did, her face would get pink with anger, and her gray eyes would sparkle; and at these signs Maura and Caroline always knew she would win the day.

"Listen to who's talking," she cried, "Dennis Cafferty himself. And how old was I when you asked me to marry you? Seventeen if I was a day. And yourself only twenty and you hadn't even finished serving your time."

Caroline saw Daddy looking at Mum; his glance became admiring, his expression softened, he began to smile and then to laugh.

"Nora, my love, you have me there. You're a devil, so you are. Seventeen you were, God help me, and you're as pretty now as you were then."

To Caroline's enormous surprise and bewilderment everyone suddenly began laughing. Daddy kissed Maura. "You could hardly learn caution from the pair of us, could you, my lassie?" he laughed. Then he shook hands with Geoff. "She's a devil, just like her mother, and don't say I didn't warn you."

He went to the cupboard and brought out two bottles, one of sherry and one of whisky, which he kept for special occasions, and four small glasses with gold rims. He poured out sherry for Mum and Maura and whisky for himself and Geoff.

"What about me?" squeaked Caroline, bouncing up and down on her chair with excitement.

So he fetched another glass and poured out a tablespoonful of sherry and added water.

"If it's engaged you are we must drink to you both," Daddy said. "Here's to your health and happiness and may you have a long life to enjoy them in." He downed his drink and poured another. "And now you must drink to your mother because she's saved me making a fool of myself more times than I can count."

Caroline sipped her sherry and water which tasted quite horrid. She thought about another slice of chocolate cake to take the taste away and decided that no one would notice.

Daddy kissed Maura again.

"Now you two can run off to your gallivanting," he said, "because I want an hour to myself to read the papers. And mind you remember, I don't want to hear anything about weddings until Maura's through university."

11

At the end of June, Maura, with whoops of joy, left high school forever and ever. She still had to wait for her exam results but she wasn't really worried. Dad nearly burst himself with pride because she was top of the school along with a perfectly terrible boy called Robert Wilkinson, who was going to be a minister and was always trying to involve her in jolly cocoa parties. She won an essay prize as well about Jane Austen's heroines; somehow she seemed to understand them better since she had known Geoff. So Dad purred and glowed, arranged her prize books in a special place in the bookcase and put her picture from the evening paper in his wallet — doubtless to bore his friends with, Maura thought, but she didn't really mind.

Linda was third in the class and at the prize-giving she gave a recitation from *Twelfth Night,* the speech beginning "Make me a willow cabin at your gates," which brought the house down. Maura still thought she ought to go to Drama College, but Linda said Edinburgh University had a super dramatic society. If she joined that she'd maybe get a part in a fringe play at the festival and her parents would change their minds about acting and striptease.

She and Maura had both got their Marks and Spencers jobs but they decided to have a fortnight's vacation first. Maura hadn't really wanted to go to the cottage with the rest of the family but she had no money to do anything more exciting, and anyhow Geoff wouldn't be free. So she consoled herself with the thought that she could lie in the sun and work up a nice tan and read and generally laze about. Geoff had just started buying a scooter on the installment plan, and he'd been invited to come and join them whenever he could. With Geoff, even fishing might be fun. And she would only be at the cottage for a fortnight; after that she and Dad would come back to Edinburgh, leaving Mum and Caroline behind for the rest of the summer.

Dad and Caroline were naturally jumping with joy at the prospect of a summer in the country. Dad had been working steadily, even doing overtime, which he hated, to collect some extra money. So for once the Cafferty family was not at debt's door.

After the last day of school Maura spent the evening with Linda, and as she sat in the bus coming home, she thought how splendid everything was — her engagement to Geoff, being top of the school, the prospect of a couple of weeks' idling in the sun (if there was any sun), and then the job at M. and S. earning enough money to buy clothes before university term started. No more high school! No more school uniform! She looked out of the window and all the people in their gay summer clothes looked happy too. The bus conductor pretended to be smitten with her and held her hand passionately while he pressed the ticket into it and tried to make a date with her. Sometimes this sort of thing annoyed her, but tonight she just laughed and kidded him back.

Mum was ironing Caroline's clothes when she got back and they started having a cozy mother-and-daughter chat; Maura talked about Geoff and Mum talked about Dad.

"Where is he, by the way?" Maura asked.

"Oh, I guess he's celebrating the vacation with his pals," said Mum, smiling, "and he deserves to."

"He feels pretty good at having fixed up a vacation for us all, doesn't he?" said Maura generously. "It's funny, the professor and him being such friends."

"It's not funny at all," Mum said indignantly. "Your father's a very exceptional man. I often think," she sighed, "that he's not had the chance he deserves. He's the sort of man who ought to have been a Member of Parliament or an opera singer or an inventor or something."

Maura nearly laughed — Dad, an opera singer — but she saw what her mother meant, especially when she compared Dad with soggy, gray-haired, middle-aged fathers like Geoff's and Linda's.

At that moment they heard his key in the door. Mum began to put away the ironing because he hated to see her working late at night and it might spark off an argument about whether or not she ought to have an outside job.

Maura, herself, was all in favor. Mum was good at her job, she enjoyed it, and she seemed much more self-confident and cheerful since she was earning money.

Dad walked very slowly into the kitchen and at once Maura knew something was wrong. It wasn't that he was a little bit drunk; it was the expression on his face. He growled a greeting, sat down with a bang at the kitchen table, and held his head in his hands.

"The vacation's off," he said in a choked voice.

"Dennis, what's the matter? What's happened?"

"That boss fired me. Excess staff, that's what I am."

"You didn't walk out?" asked Mum nervously.

"No, I did not. I'm not needed. Not needed!" he spat out the words. "You'll have to go away without me."

"We'll do no such thing."

"I'll have to stay in Edinburgh to sign up and collect my unemployment money and fix myself up with another job."

"You can collect the money in Kelso. Now, tell us exactly what happened."

So Dad told them, not in the way he usually told stories with dramatic exaggerations and "he saids" and "I told hims" but sadly and limply. Maura felt really sorry for him.

Apparently, when they gave him his pay they had just told Dad that he needn't return after the vacation.

At first he couldn't believe it. He tackled the foreman and the works manager, and they had just said, "Sorry, Cafferty, cutting down on staff, no complaints about your work, blame the government."

"And I voted for the government," Dad said angrily. "I can tell you that there'll be one M.P. declared excess at the next election. Ach, politicians are all the same; they'll promise you anything at election time. It must be a fine job, sitting on your fat bottom in Westminster and voting more money for yourself and a freeze and a squeeze for the rest of us poor devils."

Mum made soothing noises of agreement and began making tea.

"What we need in Scotland is a few men like Kevin Barry," Dad went on, "instead of a lot of time-servers, and toadies."

Maura wondered if he'd start singing:

> Lads like Barry are no cowards,
> From the foe they will not fly,
> Lads like Barry will free Ireland,
> For her sake they'll live and die.

But he didn't. She guessed he'd probably already sung it in the pub.

"It's the injustice of it," Dad shouted, banging his fist on the table. "More productivity, they say, work harder, they say, and then — the sack. I've worked hard all summer, done overtime, the lot, and I've kept my temper, though let me tell you it's been tried often enough. And what reward do I get? I'm laid off."

"You'll find another job," said Mum, pouring him a cup of tea. "You always do."

"I won't at vacation time. And how can I go away with an easy conscience without a job to come back to?"

"You're coming with us on Monday," said Mum firmly. "I won't have the girls disappointed."

"They won't care."

"Oh, Dad, of course we will," Maura put in. "We can't possibly have a good time without you." And it was true, she thought; Dad not only enjoyed himself but made everyone else enjoy himself too.

"I'm not going."

"Dennis Cafferty, stop talking like that," Mum said. "I won't go away without you and that's flat. I've saved my wages since I started working, and for once you can stop being Father Christmas to us all and let me help out."

"I won't touch a penny of your money," retorted Dad with spirit.

"Then you'll find an odd job or two while we're away," said Mum, wisely deciding not to press her point.

Dad gulped a mouthful of tea but he refused to be cheered up.

"I'm no good," he said. "My life's a failure. I'm a hollow man."

"Oh, for goodness sake, that's just the whisky talking. Drink your tea and go up to bed."

"Look at me," Dad exclaimed, but Maura could tell he was beginning to enjoy his misery. "Thirty-nine years old and what have I got to show for it? I've never done anything. I should have gone to night school. I should have emigrated. I should have traveled round the world.

Maura," — he took her hand — "you're a clever girl. Have more sense than your old Dad and make something of your life."

"Oh I will, Dad," Maura said, playing up. She exchanged a secret wink with Mum because they both knew that now the crisis was over.

"And you're bonny as well as clever," Dad went on sentimentally, "just like your mother was at your age. Caroline's going to be a beauty too."

"We're all beautiful," said Mum crisply, "so stop feeling so sorry for yourself and go to bed. You'll feel more like making plans in the morning."

"I shall stay in Edinburgh and find another job and do without a vacation," repeated Dad, but there was a more cheerful look in his eye as he got up from his chair and squared his shoulders.

Mum kissed him good night and Maura did too, although she did not like the smell of whisky.

"Two beautiful girls," he said and swayed out of the room.

Mum laughed softly. "He'll come," she said, "but he's going to need an awful lot of persuading."

12

Caroline went back to school in the last week in August. During the summer she had grown one and a half inches and put on four pounds, and after many exclamations about her fantastic rate of growth, Mum had bought her a new school blazer, a new pleated skirt and new shoes. So Caroline felt very self-conscious and well dressed.

One of the first things she had had to do at school was to write a composition about her vacation, and for once she felt she could compete with the other girls.

"My Dad and Mum and my big sister and me stayed in a cottage in the country," she wrote, "and I did lots of gardening and caught a fish. I had it fried for my tea. One day we took a bus and went to visit a ruined abbey. Monks used to live there. I climbed up a little twisty staircase to the top of a tower. The river there is called the Tweed."

She paused. How difficult it was to describe a holiday. All the smells and colors and conversations were in her head, but she couldn't put them down in words.

"In the evenings we played racing demon and my Dad always won. The cottage belongs to a professor and my Dad put in the electrissity as he is very clever with electrissity." There, that would have to do.

But she had left out about going for the milk every morning before breakfast, and the farmer's wife letting her feed the calves and how the littlest calves had licked each other's faces when they had finished their milk; how she had chosen brown eggs; how she had found a hedgehog in the garden. She had left out how they had teased Maura for spending most of her time writing long letters to Geoff and refusing to go out before the postman had come. She had left out about falling into the stream and hurrying home with her boots going *squelch squelch* at every step.

It had all been super and marvelous, and yet there had been something not quite satisfactory about it. Somehow Dad had not been so gay as he usually was. He had had an odd way of looking at Geoff, who did come to visit them on his scooter, and had kept on saying with a sarcastic edge to his voice, "I suppose you two will want to go off on your own." And he kept going on, too, about the government which he usually described as "that lot down in Westminster." He seemed to spend a lot of time gazing moodily out of the window and then without a word to anyone would suddenly stride out of the house for long solitary walks. And he had started talking about himself as an old man. "But, Daddy, you're not old," Caroline would protest.

"Can't you see me gray hairs?" he would say, and then Caroline would have to make an intensive search in his thick dark hair and report that there wasn't a single one.

Mum, on the other hand, had never appeared so jolly and cheerful. She had always been ready for expeditions, with delicious picnic meals, prepared at a moment's notice, and she had not bothered about Daddy's odd moods. She just tried to be particularly gentle and tactful to him, rather as if he too were her child.

"Caroline Cafferty," said the teacher, "stop dreaming and get on with your work."

Caroline sighed. She was in class five now and teachers were beginning to talk ominously about exams. Moreover, since she had gone back to school, Daddy had begun asking her searching questions about her progress, and who was likely to be top of the class in the end-of-term exams. He scoffed at the books she liked reading, which he said were babyish, and chose books for her from the library which were full of long boring descriptions.

Caroline liked to tell him quite different things about school — whether Miss Smith could possibly be a witch in her spare time, swooping over the school on a broomstick; whether the math teacher could be going to have a baby — she was getting awfully fat; how a black cat had mysteriously appeared in the classroom; how they were growing hyacinth bulbs in glasses of water, and how she might be going to be an angel in the Christmas play. But Daddy brushed all this information aside, exhorting her once again to work hard and get near the top of the class. "Your old Dad may not be much of a scholar," he would say deprecatingly, "but he's got two clever daughters."

Caroline wriggled with embarrassment, for she knew quite well that she wasn't clever; she had never been top in a single exam and had been near the bottom in one or two. She didn't like the way Daddy examined her books, and she felt so nervous doing her homework under his anxious eye that she began lying and saying she hadn't any. She felt it was easier to bear the teacher being cross.

The only person who might have been sympathetic was Maura. She was quite grown up now, dashing in and out of the house wearing a huge college scarf and talking in a superior way about "the lousy lecturer in moral philosophy" and what "her" professor had said. The rest of her conversation was all about Geoff. She seemed no longer to have time for cozy bedtime chats with Caroline.

When she eventually got her report card Caroline realized that it was even worse than she feared. She had dropped from eighth in the class to fifteenth, and the teachers' comments had an awful similarity: "Must try harder," "Has not worked well this term," "Must learn to concentrate," and even "Poor." What would Daddy say? The card lay like a guilty secret in the bottom of her satchel. Caroline was tempted to tear it up and pretend she had lost it. She dawdled home although a gale was blowing, finely laced with icy rain. She wanted to be cold and wet and miserable so she took particular pains to step in all the puddles in order that her feet would be cold and wet as well. She looked at the bare spiky branches of the trees writhing in the wind like black snakes, the sodden, grayish-colored grass, and even thoughts of Christmas failed to cheer her up.

"Good gracious, Caroline, imagine walking home on a day like this," Mum said angrily. "You're wet through."

"I lost my bus money," mumbled Caroline.

"You're a careless, silly child."

"So what?" said Caroline rudely.

Mum made an exasperated face. "Go up and change this instant."

Caroline stumped out of the room sulkily, took off her wet clothes, and purposely left them lying in a crumpled heap on the floor. She took the report card out of her satchel and hid it under her socks and underwear in the top of her chest of drawers. She would think what to do about it later. Then she stumped into the bathroom and dried her hair, purposely leaving the wet towel on the floor too.

"Give me your wet clothes and I'll hang them up to dry," said Mum.

"I'll get them after tea."

"You'll get them this minute."

"Oh, all right, don't go on and on."

She handed Mum the bundle without a word and sat down at the table.

"I can't think what's come over you lately," complained her mother. "What's the matter?"

So much was the matter that Caroline did not reply. She put both her elbows on the table, held her cup of tea in both hands, and slurped noisily.

"Caroline, table manners!"

Caroline scowled.

Daddy arrived home wet through too and in an equally nasty temper. He was now working for a building firm on a new housing scheme, and he grumbled incessantly about overtime and skimped work.

"Cartwrights is the meanest firm in Scotland," he spluttered. "Coining money by the bucketful and too mean to give their workers a decent shelter. There we are, forty of us tradesmen, crammed into a dirty chicken coop, with a miserable stove that just about raises the temperature to zero and not even room enough for us all to sit down."

"Disgraceful," Mum agreed.

"If we were animals there'd be nationwide protests, but we're only human beings."

"Have you complained?" asked Mum nervously.

"Complained? I've yelled my head off about it but the fellows are so gutless they won't stick their necks out — all too scared of getting laid off just before Christmas."

"Have your tea, Dennis," Mum said, as if she hoped that he would also be gutless and not stick his neck out before Christmas.

"I'll have to change first. And the mud on the site — just look at these shoes?"

Mum looked and sighed, for a good part of the mud was now on her kitchen floor but she choked back what she clearly wanted to say. Caroline, remembering the summer when he had been out of work and everyone had been cross and talked about money all the time, said self-righteously, "Gosh, just look at the mud Dad's left on the floor."

"Keep your mouth shut if you've nothing pleasant to say," retorted Mum.

But when Daddy had changed into warm dry clothes, toweled his hair until it stood on end and eaten a large plate of sausages, baked beans and chips, his spirits improved.

"How's my girl?" he asked Caroline. "Brought your report card home yet?"

Caroline shook her head. She couldn't bring herself to speak.

"When are you getting it?"

"I dunno."

"Caroline's in a bad mood," Mum explained.

"Why are you always picking on me?" flashed Caroline.

"You're either in a bad mood or you're sickening for the flu, and in either case you'll be better off in bed."

Caroline knew it was no use arguing when Mum used this particular tone of voice, and went to her room. She looked at her report card again. No, she simply dared not show it to Daddy. She climbed into bed, pulled the covers high under her chin, and stared resentfully at the ceiling. Perhaps she *was* going to get the flu. It would certainly make things easier. No one could be beastly to you when you were ill. Now she came to think of it she did have the beginnings of a sore throat and a headache.

Later, Mum came up with a hot lemon drink and an aspirin.

"Feeling better, dear?"

"No."

"Where does it hurt?"

"I just don't feel well."

"If you're not better in the morning you must stay in bed."

"All right."

"Good night, dear."

It was wonderful to be ill. Mum brought her breakfast in bed and took the day off work to look after her, which meant stacks of comics to read, black currant sweeties to suck, and a constant supply of hot-water bottles.

In the afternoon she came in armed with dusters, furniture polish and a bucket of hot water.

"I'll take the opportunity of giving your room a good cleaning," she said. So Caroline lay happily in bed, watching her deft movements as she dusted and replaced books, swept up dirty clothes, washed the woodwork, hung up her blazer and skirt, and arranged her shoes in a neat row.

"Now I'll do your drawers," she said briskly.

"I'll do them myself," cried Caroline, suddenly aware of her danger.

"You'll do no such thing."

"But — "

Before Caroline could stop her, her mother had emptied the top drawer onto the floor and there, of course, lay the famous report card.

"Caroline, what's this?"

"Leave it alone," shrieked Caroline. "Leave it alone, it's private."

Mum took the report out of the envelope and read it with an expressionless face.

"Were you afraid to show it to Daddy?"

"Mmm."

"Well, it's not a very good report, certainly."

"Please don't show it to Daddy."

"There's nothing so terrible about a bad report. Everyone gets them now and again. Maura often did."

"But I'm not clever like Maura," murmured Caroline.

"Neither am I," said her mother cheerfully. "Still I think you might work a bit harder next term."

"I'll try," said Caroline doubtfully.

"Now what would you like for your tea? Scrambled egg?"

Daddy came in after tea and Caroline couldn't make out if he had seen the report card or not. Certainly he did not talk about it. He was particularly lively and affectionate, played a game with her, and told her a long fantastic story about a leprechaun who lived in a telephone box and saw to it that everyone got wrong numbers. Then he sat on her bed, told her to hurry up and get well because he needed her help in buying his presents and decorating the Christmas tree, and kissed her good night.

Caroline listened for Maura to come in and talk to her but she was always late these days.

13

The Cafferty family loved celebrations, and though most people celebrated either Christmas or New Year, they always celebrated both holidays even if they were so broke that they had to do it on sausages and ginger beer. This Christmas Eve Mum worked in the kitchen, preparing mountains of food while the enticing smell of baking filled the whole house. There were rows of mince pies on trays, a Christmas cake in a silver frill, and an extra-large chicken, already stuffed, garlanded with strips of bacon, sitting in a baking tin. Dad arrived back from work bubbling over with exuberance, carrying loads of beer cans and bottles; and right up to the last minute before the shops closed, he and Caroline kept dashing out for things they had forgotten, more Christmas paper, red candles, a box of crackers, a box of shortbread, nuts, and dates and oranges. All of them had mysterious packages under their beds which people were strictly forbidden to prod or even to look at.

Maura had bought a plant in a pot for Mum, a cuddly mohair scarf for Caroline, a green tie for Dad in honor of old Ireland, and for Geoff she'd bought a wallet made of real pigskin.

She helped Dad and Caroline decorate the

tree and cut out some little gold paper angels as well as some rather modish arrangements of holly and scarlet ribbon. Dad, of course, fixed the lights.

"Mustn't forget the mistletoe for Geoff," he said, giving her a sly look, as he attached a bunch of mistletoe to the ceiling light in the hall. "Pass me the scissors, Caroline." As if Geoff needed the inspiration of mistletoe!

"Are we going to sing some carols?" asked Caroline.

"Of course, run and tell your mother."

Carol singing was another thing the family did and Maura enjoyed it in spite of herself. Fortunately they could all sing in tune. So they went into the front room and sang "Holy Night," "The Holly and the Ivy," and "Unto Us a Babe Is Born," with Caroline and Mum singing the tune, Dad providing rather a fine tenor, and Maura trying out some of the descants she'd learned at school.

"We're good enough to be professional," said Dad smugly, and even Maura thought that they weren't at all bad.

Then came the business of hanging up stockings. Of course Maura was too old, but she played up for Caroline's sake because Caroline wasn't yet one hundred percent sure who filled them.

Dad told long complicated stories about Father Christmas and always made her put out a cookie and a small glass of whisky for him. So when they had disappeared in the morning Caroline thought it direct proof that Father

Christmas must have been there. Or maybe she too played up in order to please Dad. Mum usually put a whole lot of little things in Maura's stocking that she really needed, like a new toothbrush, a specially nice cake of soap, a new wash cloth, new stockings, and some candy. And then Caroline would come into Maura's bed in the morning to open their stockings together. After that they would go and show their loot to Mum and Dad, who would go through all the motions of being terrifically surprised. Everything had to be done in a sort of ritual, which was silly, Maura supposed, but which was much more fun than the unorganized sort of Christmas some of her friends had, opening their presents immediately instead of waiting for the proper day.

Geoff came around about half-past twelve and distributed his presents — a fountain pen for Dad, chocolates for Mum, a charm bracelet for Caroline — really thoughtful, well-chosen presents which made her very proud of him.

Maura's present was very small, which was much more exciting and mysterious than a big one would have been. Under the tissue paper was a tiny box and inside the box was an antique silver ring with a big topaz. It was absolutely fabulous and a complete surprise. Maura put it on her engagement finger and kissed Geoff hard, mistletoe or no mistletoe.

"Thank you, thank you, thank you," she said breathlessly. "Look, Dad, my ring, isn't it fabulous?"

"Very nice," said Dad, but coldly, Maura

thought, and he shot a look at Geoff as if to say, "This is *my* daughter." He'd given them all new dresses, scarlet for Caroline, dark blue for Mum, and dull purple for her, so he had nothing to reproach himself for. But naturally the ring thrilled her more than anything else because Geoff had given it to her and it meant he loved her.

"Now, how about Christmas drinks for everyone," Dad asked, recovering his good humor. He asked them what they'd like and handed the glasses round as politely as if they were company. They sat down in front of the blazing fire and Caroline babbled about her presents, insisting upon showing them all to Geoff. Then she sat on the arm of Dad's chair with her soda.

"Isn't Christmas lovely, Daddy? You do like your cigars, don't you?"

"They're grand. I'll have one after my dinner and pretend I'm a building tycoon."

"What's a tycoon?"

"Someone who's richer than I'll ever be," he said, but he didn't sound bitter. He must have felt pretty rich himself at the moment, Maura thought, with enough food and drink in the house to last them for weeks.

She snuggled up to Geoff on the sofa, admiring her ring with little sighs of rapture. She hated nasty little mean diamonds, as small as a pinhead, that most girls had for engagement rings. She much preferred the dull glow of a topaz or one of those green mossy stones like moss agate or chrysoprase. What good taste Geoff had!

After a while Mum took Caroline into the kitchen to help with the dinner and she was left alone with Geoff and Dad. She could never understand why Geoff, who was usually so gay and talkative, should suddenly become tongue tied with Dad. And Dad was the same. Now there was silence while they looked at each other with a false jocularity, then they both started to speak at the same time. Geoff blushed and apologized and Dad carried on — not that what he had to say was either interesting or important.

"Maura says you've had your first byline?"

Geoff leaped on this and began explaining.

"It was a bit of luck really. I was walking home from work one night and suddenly saw this building burst into flames. So I charged over and was able to phone through a report before anyone on the paper knew it had happened."

"Was that the fire in the furniture warehouse in the Grassmarket?" Dad asked, always hot on details.

"Yes, but luckily no one was hurt. I suppose some old night watchman had flung a cigarette end in some vulnerable spot."

There was another pause.

"Your parents keeping well?" Dad with an effort began again.

Honestly, thought Maura in disgust, he might have done better than that.

"They're pretty spry," Geoff said. "They grumble about this Christmas business, though. My mother always behaves as if she ran the whole event singlehanded."

"We've been run off our legs, too, but we enjoy it, don't we, Maura?"

"Mmm," she grunted.

There was another silence. Maura decided that she had better help Mum also, so she got up off the sofa and started arranging chairs around the table.

"Do you go back to work tomorrow?" Geoff asked, trying to keep the conversation going.

"I do and it's pure murder on the site in this weather. Might as well be out of doors."

"Are the buildings nearly finished?"

"They're due to be finished in April," said Dad.

The next silence was fortunately broken by Caroline who came in to ask Maura to help carry the dishes, and then they all sat down, Maura beside Geoff, and Dad at the head of the table patriarchally carving the chicken.

It was a delicious meal. The chicken was smooth and white, the bread sauce creamy, the roast potatoes brown and crisp, the cranberry sauce sharp-sweet, and the small green Brussels sprouts like tender leafy nuts; the Christmas pudding was fruity and black and absolutely stuffed with sixpences. I hope I'll be as good a cook as Mum, thought Maura. Not that Mum could do anything fancy, but give her meat and two vegetables or fruit pie and cream, or even ordinary hamburgers and potatoes, and everything was hot and tasty and well cooked. And she didn't make a fuss about it either. Maura hated women who disappeared into the kitchen for hours and then reappeared, disheveled and exhausted, grumbling about how they worked their fingers to the bone and expecting lyrical praise after every mouthful. Mum just took it all for granted. She looked good in her new dress, too, and she beamed around at them all as if to say what a nice family they were and how happy she was to feed them all this delicious food.

Caroline was looking pretty in scarlet, eating with enthusiasm and gazing around the table with her dreamy eyes. It was nice to have a younger sister in the house at Christmas, Maura thought, who looked at everything as if for the first time. And this was certainly a first time, the first time Geoff had been with them for Christmas.

Dad obviously fancied himself playing host. He carved the chicken with expert strokes — he was very vain about his carving and was always explaining the different methods to them — and he piled everyone's plates high without that calculating look that meant "this has got to last for tomorrow." Then he filled their glasses with red wine that "a man he had met" had sold him at wholesale prices. Maura thought it tasted horrible at first, but then she got used to the taste and rather liked it. And Geoff, who rather prided himself on knowing about things like wine, though Maura didn't think he really did, said it was an excellent young claret. Caroline had ginger beer.

Looking at Dad, flushed partly from the hot fire and partly from the wine, Maura could realize that with his glowing eyes, thick dark hair, and the quick assured way he carved or drew corks or poured wine, most people would think him attractive. If I were Mum, I'd be proud of him too, she thought. Perhaps he ought to have been an M.P. or an inventor or an opera singer. Under the influence of the wine she could imagine him in the House of Commons, making impassioned speeches about national independence, or on the stage warbling about his undying love for some beautiful maiden, or crying "Eureka!" because he had discovered how to make clothes out of grass. Maura remembered that evening when he had said that he was a failure and a hollow man, and she realized that from his point of view it was true. He did deserve something better than to be bawled at by stupid foremen or to be laid off. And she suddenly understood why he nagged her and Caroline to get educated and make something of their lives.

How different Geoff was — he would definitely make something of his life. Maura passed him the bread sauce, the cranberry sauce, the salt and pepper, smiling every time she caught his eye. She was longing to have his arm around her and to touch his rough-smooth hair, but in the meantime she was quite prepared to go through the Christmas routine, sing carols, pull crackers, play childish games, and even do her share of the chores. She felt proud that she could show him her nice, good-looking, well-mannered family and show him off to them.

After the meal was over, she helped Mum clear away and then they sat around the fire, nibbling chocolates and playing a game of donkey to please Caroline. And all the time Maura was nerving herself to make an announcement that had been weighing on her mind for weeks. Surely no one could be angry on Christmas Day? And yet she did not entirely trust Dad.

At last she dared.

"Dad, Geoff and I have something to tell you."

"Oh?" said Dad, raising his eyebrows.

"We are going to get married on New Year's Eve."

There, it was out. She found that she was trembling. She looked beseechingly at Geoff who smiled encouragement. Then she waited for the explosion.

"I see," said Dad.

"You see," she went on in a rush, "lots of students get married and it doesn't interfere with their work."

"And I've found an apartment and I'm earning reasonable money now, and Maura has her scholarship," put in Geoff.

"I see," said Dad again. The color drained from his face and he avoided everyone's eyes.

"Aren't you going to say something?" Maura pleaded. She was all ready for a row; she and Geoff had all their arguments lined up.

"No. I am not. I've said it all. You've made up your minds and that's all there is to it."

Maura felt limp with anticlimax. She would have preferred one of his typical outbursts. This cold, uninterested tone of voice chilled her to the bone. She felt that she'd stuck a knife into him and he was merely saying silently that it was sharper than a serpent's tooth to have a thankless child.

"Then it's all right?" she begged him.

If only he'd say something. She wanted to add, "And you'll come to the wedding, won't you?" but the words stuck in her throat.

"You know very well it's not all right." His voice was dead, calm, and absolutely without life or color.

"But, Dad —" She wanted to explain and justify.

"I said I didn't want to discuss it at all and I won't, least of all today when we're having a family party."

Geoff took her hand and they stood there miserably. Caroline gazed open-mouthed. She didn't even beg to be a bridesmaid. Mum did not say a word either, she just stared at the fire. The silence seemed to suffocate them.

"We'd better go, Maura," Geoff said desperately at last. "You know we promised to look in on my parents."

Dad stared into some imaginary bottomless pit. Then he got up and poured himself a hefty dram from the whisky bottle, drained it at a gulp and flung the glass into the grate. Caroline jumped, and gave a little cry of alarm. He turned to her. "Let's look at that new book of yours, Caroline," he said at last in nearly his normal voice.

Geoff and Maura fled.

In the bus she couldn't stop crying although Geoff had his arm around her, and was gentle and sympathetic.

"It's so unfair," she gulped. "How can Dad be so horrible to me?"

"Never mind, he'll come around in time," Geoff said comfortingly.

"It's not as if we were doing something wrong. Why shouldn't we get married?"

"He doesn't want you to grow up."

"Oh I know. I've got to be his clever little girl until I'm ninety-two."

"Will he relent in time to come to the wedding, do you think?"

"I didn't dare ask."

"Your mother'll fix it."

"I hope so."

"You don't want to back out, do you?" wondered Geoff. "I mean we could postpone the wedding."

"No," Maura said fiercely.

"Good. Now cheer up, darling, and mop your pretty eyes."

Maura mopped and tried to smile. After all, she was getting married in less than a week. She ought to be, she must be, happy.

They hadn't intended to get married so soon. The idea had crept up on them unawares during the last couple of months. In the summer it had been different — just being together was so surprising and exciting. If they wanted to be alone, they could go to the Botanic Gardens or wander up on the Pentland Hills. But when the cold weather came and the dark nights set in they had nowhere to go. They wandered miserably from cafés to the movies. In Geoff's house his mother was always tapping on the door, offering them food and drink, and in Maura's house the family was always there. They could only kiss on stairs and in dark doorways and in the back row of the movies, and every time they said good night it was like having a tooth pulled without an anesthetic. Finally Geoff had decided that the only solution was for him to get his own apartment; and if he did, Maura suggested, why not get married so that they could live in it together? At first Geoff had had reservations; he thought they should be free to concentrate on their work, but eventually he had agreed that all these painful farewells were even more distracting.

He had been in favor, too, of giving the parents ample warning, but Maura had pointed out that Dad would never accept the idea, and if she had to stand weeks of disapproval she would fall into a decline and have to be taken to the Registry Office in a wheelchair. So Geoff, who was very businesslike, found an apartment and calculated exactly how much they could afford for living expenses while continuing to save.

The apartment was pretty terrible, Maura thought; in fact she had nearly died when Geoff took her to see it for the first time. It was just two big rooms, with a shared kitchen and bathroom, on an old square off Leith Walk. The furniture was ramshackle; there were pink shiny damask curtains, and motheaten old rugs covered the worn places on the linoleum. Still, it would be their very own and they would soon save up for something better.

Fortunately Maura did not care about a fancy wedding with a white dress, orange blossoms, champagne, and speeches. She thought it would be much more romantic to whisk off to the Registry Office and then roar away to Gaylord Square on the back of Geoff's scooter for a gay party with just a few friends instead of hordes of boring elderly relations. Still, she had wanted Dad to be there. He was so good at parties; and she wouldn't have minded him singing for once.

During that week they went to the flat every day. Maura scrubbed and polished; they bought dish towels, egg whisks, soap powder, and glasses; they brought their clothes in suitcases. It was all terribly exciting, almost too exciting to be pleasant.

On the day before the wedding Maura went to the flat as usual. As she climbed up the now familiar dark smelly stairs and fitted her very own latchkey into the door she thought, "Tomorrow this will be my home. Tomorrow I'll be Mrs. Geoffrey Collingwood."

Geoff was there already, and after several long kisses he handed her a parcel. "Look, darling," he said triumphantly, "a real bargain."

Buying one's own dish towels was exciting but this sounded like something really special. Maura eagerly undid the parcel to find a collection of cutlery, just perfectly ordinary plated cutlery, without everything even matching.

"Twenty-five shillings," said Geoff, beaming.

Maura was horrified. She had set her heart on stainless steel with polished wooden handles and she'd been hoping against hope that they would get some as a wedding present. Geoff's parents, however, had given them sheets and blankets, and her parents hadn't given them anything.

"But . . ." she stammered, "you know what I wanted."

"I know, but look at the price of the fancy ones, ten shillings for a single knife."

"I've always wanted stainless steel!" Maura said stubbornly.

"Can't do pet," said Geoff with horrible cheerfulness. "A whole set would put us in the red to the tune of twenty pounds."

"But these are horrible."

Geoff's face went cold and stubborn. "I haven't got twenty pounds to spare and that's all about it."

Maura considered she had been very brave and broadminded about furnishing the flat. She had not spent a penny on anything that wasn't absolutely essential but she really needed those knives and forks.

"All right, I'll buy them myself out of my scholarship money," she cried.

"You won't," he retorted. "We've got to save."

Looking at him reproachfully, she saw once again the stranger she had seen that time in the Meadows. The Geoff she knew and loved had disappeared behind a mask. Her eyes filled with tears. If only Dad behaved like a proper father he would have bought them for her. She could hear his voice saying, "Nothing's too good for my clever girl." But failing Dad, Geoff ought to have realized how important it was for a girl to have one or two really nice things.

Geoff walked over to the window and stared

out into the square where some black leafless trees stood engraved on a blank gray sky. Even his back looked hostile.

"Savings are to spend on things you want," Maura said desperately.

"Look," said Geoff, turning around, and his voice was reasonable although his face wasn't. "We want to have a decent place of our own and we'll never get one if we don't start saving now. We have to do things gradually because we've no money and no relations to shower us with rich gifts. If you don't want to get married on that basis then we'll call the whole thing off."

"You mean *you* want to call it off."

"I don't mean anything of the sort."

"Yes, you do."

"You're being childish and ridiculous."

He flung her a glance of positive dislike and without a word strode out of the apartment.

Maura couldn't believe it. For a moment she wanted to scream. Then she rushed to the window and craned her head out to see Geoff as he stepped into the street.

"Geoff, Geoff," she yelled. She didn't mind what the neighbors thought. "Please, Geoff!" He looked up.

He paused and then his face changed and he turned into the main door again.

Maura could hear him rushing upstairs; in a second he had caught her in his arms and was hugging and kissing her.

"Darling, I'm sorry," he murmured into her neck.

"Oh, so am I."

"It was all my fault."

"No, it was mine."

"I want you to have everything you want, you know that," he said.

"Yes, I know."

"I'll get them if it's so important."

"No, it isn't important at all."

Nothing was important except getting married to Geoff.

14

Caroline hardly saw Maura that week, and when she did Maura was distant and distracted, always rushing in and out of the house with parcels and suitcases. Caroline was bitterly disappointed that there was not to be a fancy wedding: no new dress, no party, and no excitement. She tried to comfort herself by painting a picture of what a wedding should really be like: a church with a pointed spire, a bridegroom in black with a flower in his button hole, a bride with a white veil and a fluffy white gown, bridesmaids with bouquets, crowds of people throwing confetti, and a big black car festooned with white streamers. She couldn't understand why everyone was so cross about Maura getting married. Surely getting married was lovely and made people happy, but Daddy was in one of his bad moods and Mum wasn't much better.

Caroline was finishing the picture when Maura returned on the night before the wedding. She looked flushed and excited and yet something in her face must have worried Mum.

"Come and sit down by the fire, dear. You look tired," she said gently.

Maura sat, but it was obvious that she found it difficult to keep still. She jumped up to comb her hair, she fiddled with things on the dresser, she filed her nails, she picked up the paper and put it down again.

At last Mum fumbled in her bag and handed Maura an envelope.

"This is a wedding present," she said in a strange voice. "You must be needing things for the apartment."

Maura opened the envelope and her face went pink.

"Mum, twenty pounds! Oh, you oughtn't."

"They're my wages and I can spend them how I want," Mum said sharply.

Maura's eyes filled with tears and she put her arms around Mum and hugged her.

"I'm going to buy some gorgeous cutlery with it, stainless steel with polished wooden handles." Then she paused. "Mum, you are coming to the wedding, aren't you?"

"If you want me to."

"Of course I do. Twelve o'clock, tomorrow. You know where the Registry Office is?"

Caroline had stopped painting. "What about me?" she asked.

"What about you?"

"I want to come to the wedding."

"Oh, Mum, let her come. Please bring her."

"All right," Mum agreed, smiling.

Caroline considered her picture. It wasn't what she had intended but then pictures never were, any more than compositions.

"Could I give it to you as a present?" she asked Maura doubtfully.

Maura went over to examine it. Usually she

was pretty rude about Caroline's artistic efforts but this time there was a catch in her voice when she said, "It's lovely."

"Would you like it? To hang on the wall? In your new house?"

"We'd love it."

Caroline looked at her narrowly. So often grown-ups pretended that they liked things, but Maura did sound sincere.

"Do you really like it?" she persisted.

"Would I say so if I didn't, stupid?" Maura said.

Caroline was satisfied.

When Daddy came home, both Caroline and Maura looked at him appealingly, but he just sat down without a word. Maura sighed and said, "I'm going to bed," and Caroline, though she had wanted to show him her picture, decided to go too.

As Caroline lingered in the hall after brushing her teeth, she heard Mum say, "But, Dennis, you've made your point. You must come. The child will be heartbroken." And Daddy's reply, "I'm not coming! That's flat. I'm not going to condone attempts at suicide."

"You're talking nonsense, Dennis."

"All women get sentimental when it comes to weddings, but I'm not sentimental. I'm a man of principle."

Caroline crept into bed. She wanted to talk to someone, but there wasn't anyone to talk to and she was too old for George.

In the morning the atmosphere was taut with suppressed excitement. Maura wore her Christmas dress and a new white wool coat, and looked, Caroline thought, grown-up, unfamiliar, like a picture in a magazine.

Caroline held Mum's hand tightly as they walked to the Registry Office. There was Geoff, also looking grown-up and unfamiliar, in a dark suit, with his hair brushed very smooth. And there was Linda, whom Caroline knew, and a strange young man called Gordon who made supposed-to-be funny remarks about having forgotten the ring, which he referred to as "the wee golden fetter." And there were Geoff's parents, his father fat and smooth and dark-suited, and his mother in a flowery hat and black gloves, saying, "They're such children really," and "What a sweet girl Maura is," and "You must come to tea some weekend," and "We're so sorry Mr. Cafferty couldn't come," and "Of course, Geoff's got a great future in front of him."

And they both asked Caroline the usual questions, how old she was, and where did she go to school, and what did she feel about having a brother-in-law?

Geoff and Maura did not join in these conversations. They sat side by side in the little waiting room, knee by knee, hand in hand, glancing and speaking in unison, as if they were puppets worked by the same strings.

Suddenly there was silence as the clerk came in and told them to go into the inner room. They all trooped in and sat down on uncomfortably hard wooden chairs, Maura and Geoff and Linda and Gordon in front, and Mr. and Mrs. Collingwood and Caroline and Mum behind. The Registrar was short and fat and cheerful with a gay pink carnation in his buttonhole. He beamed at them all, and then started reading in a fat, jolly voice; Geoff and Maura said "I do," and Caroline, looking sideways at Mum, saw her eyes fill with tears. She gripped her hand convulsively. This was it. This was a wedding. How peculiar and mysterious and unsatisfying. There were kisses and handshakes all around, and then Maura and Geoff climbed onto the scooter and roared away. The rest of them gathered on the pavement outside the office in one of those awkward assemblies where everyone wishes to be elsewhere but is anxious to be polite.

Gordon, who apparently worked on the same paper as Geoff, went up to Linda. "Well, I must away and compose an epithalamium for the happy pair," he told her. "See you this evening." Linda replied, "Yes, I'll be there," and they looked at each other, unable to decide whether to shake hands or not. Gordon then shook hands with all the parents as if he were doing them a great favor, and walked off with a long-legged superior stride to his newspaper office. Linda lingered by Mum, obviously wanting to say something but not knowing what. She looked very pretty and blond, Caroline thought. Eventually she murmured, "I'll come and see you soon," and smiled at everyone and also disappeared into the crowd.

"Oh, I always cry at weddings," said Mrs. Collingwood, putting a small white handkerchief into her enormous handbag, "if only they knew all we know!"

140

"Would you care for a refreshment of some sort?" said Mr. Collingwood; "My wife and I would be delighted — lunch perhaps? These young things have it all their own way nowadays — sorry we've never had a chance to get together. . . ."

Mum smiled evasively. "No, Caroline and I have to get back, thank you all the same. Some other time. Come on, Caroline, say good-bye."

Caroline said good-bye. She was disgusted with the whole lot of them. If only Daddy had been there he would have known how to behave, how to turn the whole affair into a proper celebration. She trotted beside her mother wanting to ask a great many questions, but Mum's face discouraged her.

"We'll drop into the café for lunch as a treat if you like," Mum said at last. And they turned into the café that Caroline had heard so much about. As soon as they had sat down the manageress came over and spoke to them, asking once again, "And what's your name, dear?" and "Where do you go to school?" and "How old are you?" and "Isn't she a pet?" before she signaled the waitress who brought them big platefuls of roast turkey. Here Mum cheered up a little; she called the waitress by her Christian name, praised the food, and kept asking Caroline whether it was not delicious.

After the turkey they had raspberry sponge cake with cream and ice cream, and coffee, and as they left Mum smiled at the waitress and said, "I'll be back at work the day after tomorrow."

"Happy New Year to you, Mrs. Cafferty," waved the manageress in her tight black dress.

"Happy New Year," Caroline and Mum called back.

The first thing Caroline noticed when they got home was that her picture was still lying on the table.

"Oh, Mum, Maura's forgot my picture."

"Never mind, dear, you can take it there yourself later in the week."

"Do you know where they live?"

"Of course. And there's a direct bus so you can go on your own."

"Are they properly married, Mummy? I thought there'd be lots of people and confetti and —" Her questions came in a rush, "Did you like Geoff's mummy and daddy? I thought they were awful. How is Geoff my brother-in-law, does that mean he's a sort of brother? I'd like to have a brother. When will Daddy come? Can I sit up with you and watch the New Year in? You promised I could last year."

"We'll see," said Mum. "Now, Caroline, you and I have a lot to do to get everything ready for tonight. And the first thing is to clean the windows."

Daddy came in late. He was very gentle and polite, and said that of course Caroline could stay up; she was a big girl now.

15

Being married to Geoff was just as marvelous as Maura had imagined. The wedding itself had been rather a strain, but she knew she had looked nice and that was always a comfort. The party in the evening, however, had been a complete success. They had Geoff's record player and lots of people brought records. Jimmy, a friend of Geoff's, brought a guitar which he could actually play quite well, and Linda gave a hilarious takeoff of what the lady adviser at school would have said if she'd been at the wedding. They danced and sang and drank Coke and wine and beer, and Maura served cold chicken, salad, and lots of sandwiches and cake. At midnight they linked hands in the sentimental Scottish way and sang "Auld Lang Syne" and everyone kissed everyone. The only person Maura did not like much was Geoff's friend Gordon, who kept making such snide remarks as "another good man gone," and "you should love 'em and leave 'em like I do," and "I'm not going to put my head into the noose for a good few years yet." Maura supposed he meant to be funny but she hated it when men talked about marriage in that way. After all it was generally the man who proposed, and she was sure there were just as many male bullies as female bullies. In any case she and Geoff were different, and she did not like the implication that she had had to coax or bully him into doing her a special favor. She pitied the girl Gordon would eventually marry and told him so.

"Nonsense," said Gordon, a little nettled. "She'll do as I say and love obeying her lord and master. That's what women really like. Down with all this equality."

"The only people who don't want equality are the people who are afraid of it," jeered Linda. "You know you wouldn't come out of it so well, Gordon. You're just a wee frightened man underneath."

"Try me," boasted Gordon.

Linda gave him one of her searching looks which implied, "I can pick and choose and I wouldn't pick or choose you in a hundred years." How clever and charming and pretty and nice Linda is, thought Maura. I do hope she finds someone as marvelous as Geoff.

After they had toasted the New Year, everyone started tactfully getting ready to go, and they all said it had been a fabulous party and they would come again soon. They had all brought presents — a plant in a pot, a table lamp, a set of guest towels, a casserole and a carving knife and Maura felt quite sentimental about what nice friends they already had.

Then, when they had all trooped away down the stairs Geoff turned to Maura and kissed her.

"Well, Mrs. Collingwood?" he said.

"Well, Mr. Collingwood," she replied, feeling

like the Jane Austen heroines who always called their hubsands Mister — she never could imagine Elizabeth calling Mr. Darcy "Fitzwilliam."

"I love you," Geoff said.

"Oh, so do I," Maura said, "you, I mean."

She loved everything about him. She loved the way he sprang out of bed in the morning, flinging the bedclothes aside and dashing to the window to see what sort of day it was; and the absurd way he got dressed, putting on his trousers first and then having to stand with his legs apart so that they wouldn't fall down while he put on his shirt and tucked it in. She loved watching him sling his tie around his neck, and his look of concentration as he tied it and pulled it into place. She loved the way he washed his face, sloshing it with soap and water and then groping for the towel with his eyes closed. She loved watching him shaving and the smell and feel of him when he was newly shaved.

She loved the way he ate toast and marmalade, putting little bits of butter and dabs of marmalade separately on each mouthful and then discovering after he had eaten the toast that he had some butter or marmalade left over so that he had to have a new piece of toast to finish it up.

After their lovely breakfasts Geoff would set off for his office, coming back several times to tell her how much he loved her, and when to expect him home. Then Maura would be on her own. She washed and dried the dishes and put everything away, and then she went shopping, coming back to the apartment to make herself a sandwich lunch. Geoff, she discovered, was very particular about his food. He didn't like ordinary things like hamburgers or sausages. He wanted spaghetti and steak and rice and salads with French dressing. Maura bought cookbooks and struggled with complicated recipes which did not always turn out successfully, whereupon Geoff would look so rueful she would have to hug and kiss him back into good humor.

He usually did not get back home until late, except on his days off, and Maura took particular trouble to be nicely dressed and made up, with something good to eat ready prepared, just as the magazines said she should.

In the afternoons she studied, but she found she spent more time lying on the bed, gazing into space, and thinking how marvelous marriage was.

Before she went back to school, Caroline came to bring her funny picture which she hung on the wall. Maura was glad to see her and they sat beside the fire eating hot buttered toast while Caroline asked questions and listened, fascinated, to all the details of Maura's new life.

"How's Dad?" Maura asked at last, casually.

"He's got a cold."

"Is he in bed?"

"Oh no, just snuffling. He doesn't shout so much," she volunteered.

"Old age," said Maura flippantly.

"Daddy's not old. He hasn't got a gray hair. I looked," said Caroline indignantly.

So Maura told her how Geoff was being allowed to specialize in municipal affairs — of course Caroline didn't understand, but it was nice to talk about it. But Maura did not talk about the complicated family situation since she did not want Caroline to be involved. And it was complicated. Geoff had refused to visit her home while Dad was being so unpleasant, although he said she must go home whenever she wanted. But she did not want to go without Geoff. And it was the same for Mum — she wouldn't come and visit without Dad. If Caroline realized how odd it all was, she did not mention it; she just admired everything, the new blankets and glasses, and the beautiful new cutlery. Maura gave her money and when she had gone, found herself crying a little. If only Dad would relent!

Then the spring term started, and Maura found it was a great strain, trying to fit in lectures and essays with being a wife. She had to dash out of the house for 9:30 lectures just when Geoff was getting up, because he didn't start work until eleven or twelve. It was a long, long day without him, and when he did get home they would stay up until all hours, eating and talking and drinking coffee. Then of course she would sleep late the next morning and drag herself out of the house, sleepy, bad-tempered, and without having had any breakfast. Sometimes she skipped the early morning lectures in favor of an extra hour in bed and a leisurely breakfast with Geoff.

And when Geoff had a day off during the week it was terribly tempting to take a day off too, and sometimes she did. She kept promising herself that she would turn over a new leaf and do some concentrated work before the end-of-term exams, but it was so much more pleasant to spend the time with Geoff. They had friends in, they played records, they went to the movies, and on Saturday they would eat out at the Chinese restaurant, but whatever they did was colored with the warm happy knowledge that they were really married and would never have to say good-bye again when the evening was over.

It was snowy that January and February; the trees in the square were like white velvet; the roofs a patchwork of gray and white, and the Pentland Hills were huge, misty white shapes like clouds — you could hardly tell where hills ended and sky began. They spent hundreds of shillings on the gas heater and Maura shivered in her new white coat.

One thing Maura had not realized about Geoff was that as well as being pernickety about food, he was also pernickety about money. He earned fifteen pounds a week, of which three pounds went for rent, ten pounds for housekeeping, and the rest he kept for pocket money. Maura was supposed to spend three pounds of her scholarship money and save the rest. He did not actually make her keep accounts, but when she miscalculated and had to ask him for more he looked so stern and horrified that she preferred to borrow from her savings. At first ten pounds seemed a lot of money but there were so many things she had not reckoned with, like toothpaste and soap powder; sending things to the cleaners, and stockings, that it simply dissolved. By Thursday they were down to baked beans, and Geoff hated baked beans. He would look at her so reproachfully that she would swear it would never happen again and then, to make up for her deficiencies, she would dash off and buy something extravagant like steak or pork fillet.

One Saturday that she had been expecting to spend with Geoff he was called out on a job unexpectedly, and Maura suddenly felt lonely and depressed. She decided to go and call on Linda.

Linda was just getting ready to go out, so they set off together up Princes Street as they had done in the old days examining the clothes in the windows.

"I've simply got to get some boots," Linda said. "My tiny feet are frozen, and if this weather continues all my toes will drop off with frost-bite."

"Have you any money?" Maura asked enviously.

"I've got ten pounds to last till the end of term," Linda said with a comfortable laugh, "but what the hell? I'll lead a godly, righteous, and sober life and eat at home."

"Lucky you," Maura was about to say, but quickly suppressed it — she was the lucky one.

"I need boots too," she said wistfully.

"Come on, let's be devils. We're only young once."

"No, I really mustn't."

"Well, come and help choose mine."

They went into a big shoe shop and sat down on the little velvet chairs. It was warm and scented and luxurious; the assistants scurried to and fro, and they leaned back watching the other customers — a great, fat, stupid-looking girl trying to fit her great feet into little black pointed-toed evening slippers, and a tall, bored, thin girl trying on shoe after shoe, wrinkling her face in disgust at each one.

Maura fell for an absolutely fabulous pair of boots in white leather with a front lacing, but Linda said they weren't her style, she wanted black suede.

"Try them on," she said, tempting Maura.

"Could I?" Maura asked the assistant. "Have you got them in my size — five and a half?"

She had, and Maura put them on and walked up and down the soft carpet, looking at herself in the mirror. They looked perfect with her white coat. It seemed ages and ages since she had had anything new. They cost five pounds and she knew she could not afford them. She almost gave in, and then pulled herself together.

"Take me out of here, quick," she said to Linda. "Or I'll go mad and buy them with the housekeeping money."

"Don't expect me to exert a good influence," said Linda. "Och, come on, Maura, you need boots, all girls need boots in the Arctic Circle, it's not extravagance, just common sense. You'll catch pneumonia otherwise. Geoff will understand."

Maura looked down again at her elegant legs and the thought of stepping out into the slushy street in her thin shabby shoes was unendurable.

"I'll take them," she said recklessly.

"Tomorrow the deluge," said Linda and they giggled.

They paid and walked out of the shop carrying their old shoes in paper bags. Then they could not resist going into Marks and Spencers where Maura bought a white woolen hood.

She felt on top of the world.

She was rather nervous about showing her new things to Geoff, who had been absolutely livid about the cutlery, but he told her she looked maddening and mysterious and modish — he still kept finding words to describe her — and he didn't give her an argument.

The fight happened several weeks later when the electricity bill arrived.

Although the gas fire was on a meter, the electricity was on a quarterly account and Maura was supposed to put something by each week so that she would be ready to pay it, but of course she had forgotten. It was twelve pounds ten.

"How much have we got toward it?" asked Geoff, when he'd stopped swearing at the Electricity Board and calling them robbers and bullies.

"I don't quite know," Maura hesitated guiltily.

"Maura, tell me the truth."

"I forgot," she said miserably.

"You forgot?"

"Well, there are so many things."

"It's absolutely unforgivable. Twelve pounds ten. And you go and buy boots. Not to speak of the wretched cutlery."

"I had to have boots."

"You should have discussed it with me first."

"You weren't there."

"How are we ever going to save if you're so disorganized?"

"I suppose you're sorry you married me."

"I think your father was probably right when he said you were too young."

Geoff's face had that cold distant look again that made her want to cry or scream or throw things at him.

"Show me your post office savings book," he demanded.

"I won't. It's none of your business."

Maura rushed into the bedroom and threw herself down on the bed and cried and cried. She knew it was her fault really, but she could not help feeling that Geoff was partly to blame; after all it was he who refused to eat sausages and baked beans. She heard the flat door slam. Geoff had probably left her forever and ever.

6

Caroline trotted between the two families answering deceptively casual questions — "How's Dad?" from Maura and "How's Maura getting on?" from Mum. "Fine," she always answered vaguely. She was aware that she could easily say the wrong thing to the wrong person and "Fine" seemed the easiest solution. In actual fact neither was fine.

Daddy's cold had turned into bronchitis; he had stayed in bed, gotten up and gone to work and then returned to bed again, white-faced and wheezing, blaming the conditions on the site, the Minister of Social Security, his boss, the government, or the weather, as the mood took him, but without his usual verve and explosive indignation. It seemed ages since he had thought of a new plan for making their fortunes or talked about living in a cottage in the country.

Maura wasn't fine either. Once when Caroline called, she had been tearstained and jumpy, and had talked about electricity bills, and another time about a failed exam. "Of course it doesn't matter," she explained with a certain defiance. "I can take it again in the summer, but Geoff seems to think it's the end of the world."

Geoff was seldom in when Caroline made her visits, but when he was there he always seemed to be picking on Maura, calling her a scatter-brain or criticizing her cooking or her untidiness, and Maura, instead of flying into a rage and shouting at him as she used to do at home when Daddy picked on her went pink, bit her lip, and said nothing. It wasn't like her a bit. And Geoff grumbled about the *Herald*, the lousy wages it paid, and its generally parochial character, the lack of opportunity for ambitious young journalists in Scotland, and how it was high time he was working for a decent national daily with a bit of zing to it. He referred to their apartment as a "dump," which Caroline considered rude because she thought it was lovely to look out onto the trees in the square.

"It should have been pulled down fifty years ago," snarled Geoff, "but we haven't a hope of getting a decent place at this price."

Caroline preferred it when she was alone with Maura, who enjoyed nothing better than to put away her books and make tea for them both, and tell Caroline her plans for the future. Of course they would get a new place eventually, high up in a modern house, with central heating, a streamlined kitchen, and lovely furniture. Of course Geoff would get a super job sooner or later because he was so clever and hard working. And when she had her degree she would get a super job herself and then they would have lots of money and would be able to go to Spain or Greece for their vacations. And they'd have a baby, and Caroline could come and stay and help look after her nephew or niece.

"What names do you like, Carol?"

"David," said Caroline promptly, "and Pauline for a girl."

"I think Nicholas or Veronica."

"There's a girl at school called Veronica who has freckles," said Caroline. "How many babies are you going to have?"

"Two, a boy and a girl."

"I shall be an aunt," said Caroline happily. Maura had become interested again in Caroline's affairs, and so Caroline told her about the super new English teacher.

"He doesn't bother about grammar or spelling, he just tells us to write whatever comes into our heads," said Caroline enthusiastically.

"Lucky you."

"He shows us a picture or plays us a piece of music or writes a word on the blackboard, and tells us to write what it makes us think of."

"What did you write today?"

"I wrote a poem," said Caroline proudly. "Not with rhymes and things, he says it doesn't matter."

"Can you remember it?"

"It's spring in the woods
 And the birds are singing hooray.
 Their feet make criss-cross patterns in the mud
 As they go digging for worms,"

recited Caroline rapidly, hopping around the room.

"That's nice."

"It's called 'Spring,'" explained Caroline. "There was a bit about white woolly lambs dancing but I've forgotten it. We write stories too. I'm writing one about a princess."

School had become a lot nicer now that English wasn't just reading aloud from dull books or copying things in her best writing and trying to remember that "receive" and "believe" were spelled differently. She liked writing fairy stories too, because she kept remembering bits of the ones Daddy had told her.

She took a lot of trouble with the one about the princess, sitting at the kitchen table and writing in a notebook marked *Caroline Cafferty, Secret Very Private* and refusing to let Daddy or Mummy see a word though she allowed them to advise her about spelling.

This is what she wrote:

There was a beautiful princess who had a unicorn. And her father said, "No one can marry her unless he can ride on the unicorn and gallop off with her to fairyland." Lots of suitors tried, but the unicorn was only friendly with girls, and got shy and ran away. On the Princess's birthday everyone was very excited because there was a new suitor who was specially handsome and clever and the Princess liked him best. So she tied a black thread around the unicorn's neck that no one could see and when it wanted to run away it couldn't. So the Prince was able to get on and then the Princess jumped up behind him and they galloped away and lived happy ever after.

"What's all this about unicorns," asked Mr.

Parker, the English teacher, when she showed it to him.

"They're on the coat of arms of Scotland," explained Caroline importantly, "but they're in the Meadows too, on pillars."

"It's a splendid story," said Mr. Parker. "I'm going to put it in the school magazine. What about drawing a picture to go with it?"

"I'll try," said Caroline, "but I'm not very good at drawing pictures."

She scurried home to show the story to Daddy. At last she had some good news to tell him.

"It's going in the school magazine, Daddy."

"So you're a real author?"

"It's just, it's just — " Caroline didn't know what it was, so instead she just bounced around the room happily.

"And Mr. Parker wants me to draw a picture to go with it."

Daddy read the story with a funny look.

"So they lived happy ever after?" he asked.

"Oh yes, Daddy, all princesses do."

"So they do, so they do. I'd forgotten." He coughed, apologized, and coughed again. He had gone back to work again saying there was nothing wrong with him, but Mum kept anxiously offering him halibut liver oil, hot lemon drinks, and Vicks to rub on his chest. He made a great fuss and insisted that he was perfectly all right but he kept on coughing. This evening he winced visibly each time he coughed, as though his chest hurt him, and at last Mum felt his forehead as she always felt Caroline's when she was ill, and told him she thought he had a temperature.

"Leave me alone, woman. I'm as right as rain."

"Should I not call the doctor?"

"You should not call the doctor. I won't have that man pussyfooting around me."

"Either you go to bed at once and take an aspirin or I'll call him this moment. I mean it, Dennis."

Daddy grumbled and swore but he eventually allowed himself to be persuaded into bed. Caroline filled a hot-water bottle, and Mum shook out two aspirins from a bottle. When she returned she said to Caroline hesitantly, "When are you going to see Maura again?"

"I don't know, Mummy."

"Why not this evening?"

"All right."

"Tell her — no, I suppose you'd better not."

"What?"

"I'm worried about your father. I think I ought to call the doctor, but you know Dad, he hates doctors."

Caroline pondered these two apparently disconnected remarks. Was she to tell Maura that Daddy was ill and wanted to see her? Or to call the doctor? She had a definite feeling that Mum wanted her to say or do something without being actually told to.

"I ought to stay at home and look after him," Mum said, pushing back the hair from her forehead in a worried way, "but if I don't work — "

"I'll stay home from school," said Caroline quickly.

"Certainly not, just when you're doing so well."

"I don't mind."

"But I do, and your father would have a fit. If only Maura —" She paused and looked consideringly at Caroline.

Caroline walked slowly to the bus stop feeling worried, grown-up, and responsible. After all, she was ten now, she was going to have a story in the school magazine, and Mum trusted her to do something sensible. But what?

She liked going in buses by herself, especially just after the streetlights came on. As the bus rolled over North Bridge she looked up and saw Arthur's Seat, charcoal-colored in the fading light, but really green. Would it still be green if she were walking there or did grass change color at night?

Leith Walk was brightly lit and noisy and full of people. The trees in Gaylord Square were in bud again and she could hear the pigeons cooing. It *was* a nice place to live; why did Geoff call it a dump? She pushed open the main door and walked up the stone stairs, sniffing the stale musty smell that stone stairs always have. She rang the bell outside Maura's door. There was no reply. She rang again. Finally she rattled the letterbox and shouted through it, "Maura, Maura, it's me."

She heard footsteps, and then the door opened and Maura let her in. She was in her robe, her eyes were swollen and wet round the edges, and she was mopping them with a rolled-up ball of handkerchief.

"What's the matter? Are you ill?" Caroline asked, alarmed.

"Yes — no, I mean, I'm all right, it's just —

oh Caroline," and Maura began crying. Caroline followed her into the room. Her heart began to thump.

The room was chilly and untidy, and Maura sat down on a chair and began to mop her face again. Caroline stood beside her wondering what to say. Maura was grown-up now and grown-ups weren't supposed to cry.

"It's Geoff," said Maura at last. "He's gone to London."

"Gosh!"

"He said he couldn't stand this dump any longer."

"But what about you?"

"I'm to stay until he finds a job. And I haven't got any money, Caroline."

This was so bad that Caroline couldn't think of anything at all comforting to say.

"No money at all?" she gasped.

"Not till next term's scholarship money arrives. And Geoff's been gone a week and I've only had a postcard. I don't even know his address."

"Does he know you haven't any money?"

"Of course not. I was supposed to have saved. But I never could."

"What are you going to do?"

"I don't know, oh, I don't know. The thing is I don't believe he'll send for me. I think he's fed up with me too."

"He couldn't be," said Caroline indignantly; "I mean, you're married."

"He's fed up with me," repeated Maura sorrowfully.

"You'll have to come home," said Caroline.

"I can't. What would Dad say? It would be awful."

Then Caroline realized what she had to say, something that Mum had wanted but had not put into words.

"Dad's ill," she said. "And Mum wants you to come home to look after him so that she can go on going out to work."

"Did she honestly say that?"

Caroline debated with her conscience. "Yes," she said. "She told me to come here this evening and ask you. She's worried about Dad."

"What's the matter with him?"

"He coughs all the time, and he won't stay in bed."

"But Dad's never ill."

"I know. But he is now. I think his chest hurts. He makes a funny face when he coughs."

"Do you really think I should?" Maura asked at length.

"Please come, Maura."

Maura pulled herself out of the chair and peered at her face in the mirror over the mantelpiece.

"I look a sight," she murmured. "See if you can find my comb, Caroline, or lend me yours."

"You can borrow my bug rake," said Caroline, taking it out of her inside blazer pocket.

17

Maura felt quite dizzy with relief as she set off for the bus stop with Caroline carrying her bag. She felt a bit faint, too, because she'd eaten nothing but cornflakes and bread and margarine for the last two days. Of course she could have gone to Linda or borrowed from one of her friends, but she had felt too ashamed. She and Geoff had only been married a few months, and already everything had gone wrong, and he'd walked out on her.

She kept reliving that awful morning. He'd been as silent as a clam for days, looking at her as though she wasn't there, not even kissing her good night and if she asked him what was the matter he'd just said, "What isn't?"

And then he had said, oh so coldly, "It's no good, Maura, we can't go on like this. I'm damned if I'm going to drag out my life in a dump like this, in debt and with no prospects. I'm going to London to find a better job. I'll be in touch," and had simply walked out of the house. And he had said it with such terrible finality that Maura had not had the heart to plead with him or open the window and call him back. She had just sat at the breakfast table, tears dripping onto her plate, absolutely paralyzed with misery and terror.

For the next few days she hardly dared stir out of the house for fear he would suddenly come back, and when she did go out to buy some bread and milk and baked beans she hurried home with her heart pounding, hoping against hope that he'd be back and put his arms around her and tell her it had all been a ghastly mistake.

Now, sitting on the bus with Caroline, she felt that anyhow the worst pain was over. Mum would make a fuss over her, Dad would stride around the room shouting that he'd break every bone in Geoff's body, and somehow they would find Geoff and make everything all right again.

When she opened the door Mum rushed toward her and hugged her.

"Oh, Maura, I'm so glad you've come. I felt I had to call the doctor and Dad's got pleurisy. Oh, it's such a relief to see you."

The moment she said this Maura realized she had made a mistake. She hadn't come home to be comforted. She had come home to comfort Mum and look after Dad. She was a grown-up married woman, or they thought she was. All the things she had been planning to say suddenly died on her lips. She just hugged Mum back.

"Don't worry, Mum," she managed to say.

"How good of Geoff to spare you," went on Mum, as Maura hung up her coat and followed her into the kitchen.

"Actually Geoff had to go to London," Maura said as brightly as she could, at the same time giving Caroline a warning look. "He's after a new job — and he'll probably be away for a couple of weeks, so I was all on my own anyhow."

"That's grand news," said Mum, hardly listening. "I would have stayed off work myself but you know what sick pay is like."

"Don't worry, Mum, I'll look after him. Anyhow pleurisy isn't serious these days. A few jabs of penicillin and you're as good as new."

Mum smiled uncertainly. She really has gone to pieces, Maura thought as she went into Dad's room and opened the door.

Dad was lying quite still with his eyes closed and her heart gave a terrific lurch. It was the first time she had ever seen him ill. She sat down beside him, and he opened his eyes and looked at her but without really seeing her.

"Hullo, Dad," she whispered.

"Maura," he said, "good girl."

"I've come to give Mum a hand," she said.

"What nonsense, I'll be as bright as a chipmunk in a day or two."

He shut his eyes again and his breathing was quick and shallow, and then he tried to stir himself.

"How's that husband of yours?"

"He's just fine, Dad. He's off to London after a new job."

"London?"

"I'll tell you all about it tomorrow.'

"I seem to have made a right fool of myself," Dad murmured, "and your mother would call the doctor. There's nothing the matter with me."

"See you in the morning, Dad. Sleep well."

She rubbed his cheek with her hand and left the room.

"Did you have your tea yet?" Mum asked.

"Not yet."

The moment she heard the word "tea" Maura remembered how hungry she was. Oh, the glorious thought of food!

"I'll heat you some soup and you can have an egg."

"You sit down, Mum. I'll get it."

For once Mum obeyed her and sat down wearily while Maura heated up a huge plateful of thick lentil soup with the lentils and tomato puree making it a lovely orange-pink color. Maura tried not to gulp it down too eagerly but after her third plateful, not to speak of six pieces of bread and butter, Mum raised her eyebrows.

"Have you not been feeding yourself properly?"

"Of course I have, but I didn't have much lunch today and I had forgotten what time it was until Caroline arrived."

"If you don't eat properly, you'll get ill too," snapped Mum, more like her usual self. "Now fry yourself an egg."

"Honestly, I'm stuffed. I'll just have a glass of milk."

So she sipped her milk and Mum told her everything, Dad's cough, his bronchitis, how he would go back to work, how she had tried to keep him in bed, how she had dithered about calling the doctor, how she had wanted to get in touch with her, how she was working as under-manageress now and the pay was too good to miss. "How glad I am you offered to come and help," she finished.

At this Maura looked at Caroline, who was sitting at the table painting, and she just stared back, smiling blandly. The cunning little creature, Maura thought, she asked me off her own bat. Well, she's keeping my secret, so I'll keep hers.

"I'm glad too," she said.

The next few days Maura was run off her feet. She made Dad's bed, and bought food and cooked it, and cleaned the house, and rushed to and fro with glasses of lemon barley and hot-water bottles and opened the door to the doctor. Dad was a terrible patient. He was either groaning and expecting to die any minute or shouting for his clothes and announcing he would not stay in bed another minute. So Maura was either cheering him up and telling him he would be better soon or threatening him with an instant relapse if he did not do exactly what the doctor said.

"Doctors;" he sneered, "don't know anything. This fellow'd turn me into an invalid for life."

Maura did not like the doctor much herself; he was small and gray and tubby with fish-white hands that always felt cold and clammy, and he spoke in such a low, confidential voice that he made even good news sound disastrous. He said that of course Dad would be better in a couple of weeks but that on no account was he to go back to work on a building site; he must find lighter work. Maura told Mum and they decided not to fight this battle until they had to.

When Dad's temperature was back to normal and his chest had stopped hurting, he wanted books to read, so Maura had the added chore of running out to the library every day and finding a biography of Yeats, if there was one, James Barke's novels about Burns, Lady Gregory's letters, or a book about James Connolly.

Then he started asking her about her courses at the university; he demanded to know what moral philosophy was and what she would advise him to read. So Maura got him Bertrand Russell's *History of Western Philosophy* and then at last she had some peace. Dad became so utterly absorbed that every time she came up to ask him if he wanted anything he either waved her away or began asking questions about Heraclitus and Thomas Aquinas and David Hume. It was peculiar, thought Maura, that although moral philosophy had always bored her — this was the exam she had to retake in June — she began to be interested herself. She noticed with surprise that Dad would be described by her professors as having a first-class brain; he was certainly miles ahead of some of the students, and she remembered again what Mum had said about him not having the chance he deserved.

During the day she was so busy that she could only worry about Geoff at the back of her mind, but the moment she went to bed her worries all came back. What was she going to do? If she took a job she would fail her exams and if she failed her exams she would not get a scholarship.

How could she live in Gaylord Square without any money until her grant arrived? How could she ever tell Mum and Dad the truth? Even if Geoff got a job in London would he want her to join him? And if he didn't? It did not bear thinking about. Oh when, when, would Geoff write again? Every day she managed to nip down to the apartment, or to send Caroline to see if a letter had arrived, and every day there wasn't one. She would shut herself in the bathroom to cry and then wash her face in cold water in case Dad noticed.

For the first few days Dad did not mention Geoff, and then one day when he was feeling better but not yet obstreperous enough to demand his clothes he said, "Tell me, Maura, about Geoff going to London?"

"He got fed up with the *Herald*. They only let him write miserable little stories and he's awfully ambitious."

"Will he get a job in London? What does he say?"

Of course she could not admit she had had only one postcard from him in two weeks. "He sounds hopeful; he's got interviews with people but they take time to make up their minds."

"And if he gets a London job what will you do?"

"I don't know yet, Dad."

"You'll keep on and get your degree though, won't you?" he asked wistfully.

"I suppose I might get a transfer to London," Maura said without any special conviction. Now, she thought, here comes the battle. He'll burst a blood vessel if I say I don't really care as long as Geoff and I are together.

He looked at her very sharply as if he knew what was passing through her mind and then said gently, "It's all right, love, I'm not going to bite your head off. Geoff's quite right to be ambitious and you're quite right not to stand in his way. A man who doesn't get a chance to fulfill his ambitions makes a terrible husband. You're a sensible girl."

If only, thought Maura, he knew what a very unsensible girl she had been, and for the first time she got a tiny inkling of what Geoff felt. There she had been, buying expensive cutlery and new boots, and wanting clothes and meals out, and refusing to save, and neglecting her work. I'll turn over a new leaf, she vowed, I'll work hard, I'll save, I'll never buy any new clothes again, I'll keep accounts and make Geoff realize that we can't eat steak on ten pounds a week, if only, only, only I get the chance.

"You're like your mother," Dad said fondly. "never grumbles, always make the best of things."

Maura almost giggled as she thought of the many, many times Mum had grumbled, at the top of her voice too, but she wasn't going to disturb this idyllic picture. She just said, "You're getting sentimental in your old age."

That, of course, was wrong, for Dad's face clouded and he said, "Aye, old age is round the corner. I'm forty, you know, Maura, forty." He sighed and she did not know what to say. After all, he was forty.

The battle over his job came one evening when he was sitting up reading in the kitchen, while Mum was knitting and Caroline was writing something in her notebook marked *Private*.

"Time I was back at work," Dad said, looking up from his book. "I'll go back on Monday."

"You'll not, Dennis," said Mum firmly. "You're to stay off for another week, and then the doctor says you're to find some light work."

"Light work," Dad spat. "There's no such thing."

"We won't argue about it now."

"We're not going to argue at all. I'm not a cripple either mentally or physically. I'll make up my own mind about what I do and when."

"You'll do as the doctor says."

"You think I'm an invalid. You think my life is finished. You want to keep me at home like a pet dog."

Mum flushed angrily. Caroline looked up. There hadn't been a shouting match for ages.

"I know I'm not good for much," said Dad bitterly, "but I can keep a roof over my family's head and pay the bills. You know very well what light work means — it means light pay."

Then Maura had her tremendous idea. "Why don't *you* go to university, Dad?" she asked.

"Me?"

"Lots of people do. You get a grant if you promise to be a teacher."

"Listen, love, your ignorant old Dad left school at fourteen. I haven't got any "O" levels or "A" levels or whatever you call them."

"You could get them, easily, after a few months of night school. For goodness' sake,

Dad," Maura said impatiently, "you could walk through "A" level English right now and probably history too. And you could pick up French and math in no time."

"But I'm forty," Dad said stupidly. Maura could have spanked him.

"So what? There's a student in my year who's forty-three; he used to be a miner, and he's doing honors English. You could do electrical engineering at Heriot-Watt or a teacher-training course at Moray House."

"Och away," Dad said but with less scorn.

"They're crying out for teachers," Maura said triumphantly, "and you know how good you are at teaching children. Anyone with intelligence can pass the exams — look at all the rotten teachers we have."

"Gosh, yes," said Caroline with feeling.

"So I'm intelligent, am I?" said Dad wonderingly.

"Oh, Dad!" How irritating he was. "Of course you're intelligent, even though you're talking like a moron at the moment."

Dad looked around at the family as the idea began to take hold of his imagination. Then suddenly they all began to talk at once, making plans. Dad would put an ad in the evening paper and do odd electrical jobs for the time being. He'd sit for the "A" level English and history examinations right away. He would ask Professor Oxton's advice as to what course he should take. He'd start night school. Of course he would become a teacher. He had always wanted to be a teacher, now that he came to think of it. And then the final glory broke over him.

"I could teach at a country school," he exclaimed. "They'd give us a house and we could live in the country."

"With a garden!" Caroline squeaked with delight.

"With a garden, my darlings."

Dad looked absolutely radiant. So did Mum. So did Caroline. Maura was the only one who seemed to have a flicker of doubt as to whether all this was just another of his daydreams, though it needn't be, she knew. But even if it was, it was surely better for Dad to have a daydream than sit about moaning because he was forty.

"We must celebrate, me darlin's," Dad said, going for the whisky.

"Lemon barley for you," Mum said warningly.

"Nonsense. A dram will put new heart into me."

"Just a small one then."

They all had whisky except Caroline, who had some ginger beer left over from Christmas. And then Dad, of course, burst into song:

"As once I roved out very early,
   To view the green meadows in spring,
It was down by the side of a river
   I heard a fair damsel did sing.
And I stood in completest amazement
   I gazed on that maiden so fair,
She appeared to me brighter than Venus,
   That maid with the bonny brown hair,"

172

sang Dad, looking sentimentally at each of them in turn. At the end he caught Mum's hand and raised it to his lips. And Maura felt such a pang for Geoff it was as though she'd stepped onto a red-hot coal. She shut her eyes with the pain of it and gripped the side of her chair, willing herself not to cry and spoil everything.

At that moment the doorbell rang.

"It must be the doctor. Let him in, will you, Caroline," Mum said. "And for goodness' sake hide the whisky, Dennis."

Caroline seemed to take a long time, but Dad was telling them what he would like to do to all doctors and this one in particular, so Maura didn't hear voices until Caroline opened the door and said with a funny look on her face, "It's Geoff, Maura."

Geoff came slowly into the room and stood for a moment, gazing at Maura; he looked ashamed, as if he knew he had been cruel and bad-tempered and unjust yet at the same time was glad because he was in her company again.

"Maura," he said in a choked voice. "Oh, Maura!"

She was in his arms before she had time to think. They did not need to say anything. They just clung together and kissed. The tears were streaming down Maura's face, and even Geoff looked a bit damp.

At last they broke away and Geoff recovered enough to shake hands with Mum and Dad.

"How's the wild rover?" asked Dad jovially.

"Just fine," said Geoff, "now. Absolutely and perfectly fine."

"You're just in time for a dram," said Dad,

taking the bottle from where he had hidden it on the dresser.

"We thought you were the doctor," Caroline giggled.

"Doctor?" He shot an alarmed look at Maura.

"Dad's been ill," Maura said quickly, "but he's better now. Oh, we've thousands of things to tell you."

"So have I," said Geoff, "thousands and thousands of things," but looking at Maura as if to say, "wait till we're alone."

When they had toasted Geoff's return and Dad's recovery and his plans to be a teacher, Dad said with an elaborate yawn, "come on, Nora love. Off you go, Caroline. Maura and Geoff, will you turn off the lights when you go home?"

Although there were thousands and thousands of things to ask and tell, at this moment kissing seemed more important than talking. But in between kisses Geoff murmured into her hair:

"I had to go. I felt so responsible."

"I know," she murmured back.

"I wanted to write but I couldn't — not until I had some proper news."

"You don't have to explain."

"I hated not being able to give you boots and cutlery and nice clothes."

"Silly."

"I wasn't angry with you. I was angry with me."

"I know," Maura said again.

When there was more time — and there would be years and years of time — she would ask about his new job, which she was sure he'd gotten (but even if he hadn't, she did not care); she would explain how miserable she'd been, how she would never be lazy and extravagant again, and she would describe every single tiny thing that had happened since he had been away. But Geoff held her so tightly she could hardly breathe, let alone speak. And in any case, she realized, when you are kissing it is practically impossible to speak.